D0921713

DREAMING OF LOVE

Alice first meets Leo Grant late at night in the local supermarket. Unfortunately, she is wearing bunny pyjamas and a woolly hat — not exactly the outfit she would normally choose to impress a famous American author, particularly when he is with a gorgeous redhead. Alice's five-year-old niece thinks Leo Grant is a prince in disguise, straight out of a storybook, and the mysterious redhead is hiding a deadly secret. Alice's world is about to get curiouser and curiouser . . .

Books by Fay Cunningham
in the Linford Romance Library:

SNOWBOUND
DECEPTION
LOVE OR MARRIAGE

FAY CUNNINGHAM

DREAMING OF LOVE

Complete and Unabridged

LINFORD
Leicester

First published in Great Britain in 2011

First Linford Edition
published 2012

British Library CIP Data

Cunningham, Fay.
   Dreaming of love.- -
   (Linford romance library)
   1. Love stories.
   2. Large type books.
   I. Title II. Series
   823.9'2–dc23

   ISBN 978–1–4448–1322–7

Published by
F. A. Thorpe (Publishing)
Anstey, Leicestershire

Set by Words & Graphics Ltd.
Anstey, Leicestershire
Printed and bound in Great Britain by
T. J. International Ltd., Padstow, Cornwall

This book is printed on acid-free paper

1

Alice looked up from the essay she was marking, two small lines creasing her usually smooth brow. A library was supposed to be a quiet place, and the chatter and laughter coming from downstairs was beginning to annoy her. This was the first day of the school holidays and she ought to be relaxing at home, but instead she was sitting in the public library marking essays. All she asked was a bit of peace and quiet.

Leaving her work on the table, she walked to the desk at the back of the room.

'Excuse me — can you tell me what's going on downstairs?'

The girl behind the desk looked up, a big smile on her face. 'That brilliant American author, Leo Grant. He's been giving a talk about his new book. He lives in California but he's a local boy, born right here in the village.'

Alice didn't care if Leo Grant had been born right here in the library. 'I have some work to finish. Will he be here long?'

'Oh, I hope so,' the girl gushed. 'I want to get a look at him before he leaves. All I've seen is his picture on the posters.'

With a sigh, Alice went back to her papers. School holidays meant her five-year-old niece was at home, so there was no peace to be had there, either.

Half an hour later the noise downstairs still hadn't abated; in fact it had gone up a decibel or two. She stood up and stretched, easing her aching muscles. Up until that moment she hadn't noticed the posters decorating the library walls, she had been too busy with her red pen, but now she realised Leo Grant was plastered all over the place. His picture had no doubt been airbrushed, but she had to admit he had a certain charisma. Blond hair — a trifle too long for her taste — broad shoulders, blue eyes and a killer smile. She'd never heard of him and she'd never read any of his books, but she was curious now, so she walked over to the staircase and looked down.

All she could see from her vantage point was a small crowd gathered round a table. Mostly women, she noticed. She moved down a few steps, but her view was still blocked. Glancing back at the table where she'd left her papers, she walked halfway down the stairs to a point where she could actually see the man.

His hair was more light brown than blond, but the Californian sun had added streaks of yellow gold. He was tall, standing a foot above most of the people around him, but all she could see was the top of his head. She moved down yet another step and must have made some sort of noise, because he suddenly looked up and their eyes met.

Her breath caught. His eyes were a brilliant blue and his face a pleasing mix of angles. The man was straight out of her dreams. She had thought he was a fantasy, but now he was standing right in front of her. A figment of her childhood imagination. The knight in shining armour who always rescued her from the bad things lurking in the dark.

She was about to turn away when he smiled at her. She stood transfixed for a second before pulling herself together and hurrying back up the stairs. She had a feeling that if she looked down, he would still be watching her.

Making her work last until he'd gone was no problem. She was finding it impossible to concentrate on her marking and kept making silly mistakes. It was the noise that was disturbing her, she told herself. No one could be expected to work in that racket. Once blessed silence had returned below the stairs, she managed to finish her work and drive home.

* * *

Cassie rushed to greet her as soon as she came in. 'Aunty Alice! You're home.

4

Come and watch me play my new game.'

Lauren came out of the kitchen brushing flour from her apron. There was only a five-year age gap between the sisters, but they were completely unalike. Lauren was quite tall, her dark hair short and stylishly spiky, while Alice was small and petite, with ash-blonde hair down to her shoulders.

'Dinner's nearly ready,' Lauren said. 'No time for games right now, young lady. Go and wash your hands.' She looked at her sister. 'You're later than I expected.'

'A problem at the library. Well, not a problem exactly, just a very noisy publicity stunt by some American author. It took me longer than I expected to finish marking the papers.'

'You saw Leo Grant? I read in the local paper he was giving a talk about his new book. Did you know he used to live in the village? We were in the same class at school for a while, but he was Leonard Grant then. His parents split

5

up and his mother whipped him off to America.'

Lauren untied her apron and followed Alice into the living room. 'So what does he look like now?'

Alice smiled. 'I didn't really get a good look at him, but from what I could see he's blond and beautiful with a surfer body and a Californian tan. 'Leonard' wouldn't suit him at all.'

'For someone who didn't get a good look, that's a pretty detailed description. All I can remember is a lanky kid with brown hair and spots. I don't wonder he changed his name.'

'I couldn't see him properly because he was surrounded by women.' She grinned at her sister. 'But I can tell you the spots have definitely gone.'

'So he's quite a dish now, is he?'

'You could say that.'

'Did you speak to him?'

'He was too busy with his female fan club, but as he's come back to England for some reason, I imagine he'll be around for a few weeks. You're bound to catch a glimpse of him.'

Come to think of it, Alice privately admitted, she wouldn't mind another glimpse herself.

Once the evening meal was over and Cassie safely tucked up in bed, the conversation returned to Leo Grant.

'I wonder why he's come back here?' Lauren said. 'Perhaps there's been a family crisis. Leo's father is a surgeon, works at a hospital in London. A private wing of a famous eye hospital, from what I've heard.'

'You know an awful lot about the family. I don't remember any of them.'

'Because you were only a little girl when Leo got dragged off to the States. It would have been hard for him, because all his friends were here. Last I heard, he was just beginning to make a name for himself writing American crime fiction. The sort of books with a sexy heroine and a gorgeous, crime-busting hero. That would explain all the women at the library. We do like our alpha males.' Lauren smiled. 'And I know this because women love to gossip — especially when they're having their hair done.'

'Perhaps you should write a book called *Salon Secrets*. Or how about a crime thriller called *Death Cut*?'

Lauren laughed. 'You should be the one writing a book. Mum always said you live in a dream world. Go to bed and dream about Leo Grant — unless you think the excitement might keep you awake!'

★　★　★

A lot of things conspired to keep Alice awake. Thinking about the amount of work she had to get through in the summer holiday was one of them, and how they were going to keep Cassie entertained for six weeks on an ever-tightening budget was another.

After an hour of tossing and turning, she gave up and crept into the kitchen to heat milk for a mug of cocoa. Carrying her mug into the living room, she turned the television on with the sound down low and watched two consecutive episodes of a soap she'd missed during the week.

It wasn't until she went to put the milk carton back in the fridge that she realised she'd used up nearly all the milk. There was about half an inch left — not enough for Cassie's cereal in the morning, or even Lauren's cup of tea — and her sister had someone arriving for a cut and blow-dry at eight-thirty.

Not relishing an early-morning trip to the supermarket when she'd had hardly any sleep, Alice started back up the stairs, but then realised she was being stupid. She was wide awake and the supermarket now stayed open twenty-four hours. It wasn't yet midnight and the walk would only take a few minutes. It would be silly to go back to bed now and have to get up at the crack of dawn.

She tucked her pyjama bottoms into high black boots and zipped up her leather jacket, pushing her rather messy hair into a pink woolly hat with earflaps she found lying on the hall table. She only needed milk. She'd be in and out of the supermarket in a couple of minutes. No one was going to see her.

Passing the mirror in the hall, she almost laughed out loud at her reflection. She looked like an androgynous biker from some distant planet.

Deciding a handbag would make her look even more ridiculous, she stuck her phone in one pocket and her purse in another, remembering to pick up her keys before she let herself out. It was starting to rain, more a drizzle than a downpour, but she was glad of her hat.

Surprisingly, the supermarket was quite crowded, but Alice grabbed two cartons of milk and was heading for the checkout when she spotted someone who looked familiar.

Leo Grant had his back to her, but there was no mistaking that hair. He could turn round at any moment — and there was always a possibility he might recognise her from the library. A very remote possibility, she thought, remembering her image in the mirror, but she couldn't risk it. Particularly when he had a tall, leggy redhead hanging on to his arm.

Waiting until the couple had disappeared into the next aisle, Alice made a run for a self-service till. Scanning the cartons of milk only took a second, but when she opened her purse she found she only had three twenty-pence pieces. No amount of upside-down shaking would produce any more coins. With a feeling of dread she realised she had left the little wallet with her debit and credit cards back home in her handbag.

'Are you having a problem?' a woman assistant asked. 'The coins go in that little slot there.'

Alice knew that, and that notes went in the big slot, she wasn't completely stupid. 'I don't have enough money with me. I'll have to put one of the cartons back.'

'But you've already scanned the bar code on both cartons.' The woman frowned. 'Didn't you think to check you had enough money before you scanned the items?'

Alice shook her head. The answer should have been obvious. Someone was standing behind her, waiting to use the checkout, but she refused to turn round. They would have to wait.

'You can always use a credit or debit card,' the woman suggested helpfully.

'I came out in a rush and left my cards at home. I'm very sorry. If I don't buy anything, can I just go, please?'

'I don't think so.' The woman seemed to have a permanent frown. 'The cartons have already been scanned so they'll be in the system. I can't just put them back in the cabinet. I'll have to call a manager to cancel both items.'

'I'll take care of this,' a voice behind her said.

She turned in time to see Leo Grant push a twenty-pound note into the slot on the machine. Her face was already hot from embarrassment, but now her heat level went off the register.

'Thank you — but that's not necessary. I can come back in the morning.'

'No point,' he said with a shrug. 'It's already done.' He dropped the milk into a plastic bag and handed it to her. 'I'll be in the library again tomorrow. You can pay me back then if it makes you feel better.' He smiled his devastating smile. 'By the way, I like the outfit.' With that, he turned and strolled back into the store, the redhead once again glued to his arm.

Mortified, Alice grabbed the carrier bag, but before she could leave the supervisor touched her arm, pointing to the little tray on the machine.

'Don't forget your change.'

Scooping up the coins and taking the ten-pound note the woman handed her, Alice looked at the money in dismay. Now she was going to *have* to see Leo Grant again. Letting him pay for her milk was one thing, but keeping his change was something else altogether.

On second thoughts, it might be nice

to prove she could look less like a disaster. The leather gear probably looked okay and the woolly hat was quite trendy — but the pyjama bottoms had rabbits all over them. Not exactly the look she had envisaged when she came face to face with the man of her dreams.

Once she had deposited the milk in the fridge and climbed back into bed she slept really well, only waking when her alarm went off. By the time she joined her sister downstairs, two mugs of tea steamed on the kitchen table and the toast had popped up ready to be buttered.

'Where did the milk come from?' Lauren asked. 'We were almost out.'

'We were. I drank what was left last night, so I went to the supermarket and got some more. I know you can't function in the morning without your cup of tea.'

'There was enough left for tea. I made sure.'

'Yes, there was, but I made cocoa and

used it all.' She paused, wondering whether to mention her mishap, but in retrospect it was rather funny. 'Leo Grant was in the supermarket. Actually, he paid for the milk you're drinking.'

The story only took a few minutes to tell but Lauren couldn't stop giggling.

'The hat with the ear flaps belongs to Cassie. I can't believe you wore it. You must have looked ridiculous.'

'It was raining,' Alice said defensively. 'I didn't expect to meet anyone I know, and as I don't know Leo Grant or his girlfriend it doesn't matter what they think of me.'

'For goodness' sake, Alice, you should take more care how you look. You never know *who* you'll meet. I never go out without make-up, and I always try to look my best in case I meet a client. You're a teacher, for goodness' sake. What if the paparazzi had followed Leo Grant — and took a picture with you in it?'

'I assure you none of my pupils or any of the staff would have recognised me. Like you said, I looked ridiculous.' She took a bite of toast. 'Besides, authors are fairly anonymous, aren't they? Unless you write something like Harry Potter, of course.'

Lauren shrugged. 'I must admit I don't know what any of my favourite authors look like apart from their picture on the dust cover, and that stays the same for years and years. They never get any older.' She looked at her watch. 'Can you get Cassie up for me? It's amazing, isn't it — she was always first up in the morning until she started school, and now I have to shake her awake. I know it's the start of the holiday today, but I don't want her to get into the habit of sleeping late.'

Lauren's hair salon was based in the conservatory at the back of the house. The conservatory faced east, so it didn't get too warm, even in the summer, and the plumbing left from an old outside toilet had meant that a washbasin could be installed quite cheaply. When their mother died the girls both had well-paying jobs so they could manage the mortgage between them, but Lauren's pregnancy had meant a change of plan and they had decided to have the house adapted so she could work from home. With Alice at home in the school holidays, it all worked quite well — apart from the fact that there were always bills to be paid, and never enough money left for emergencies.

Alice found Cassie sitting up in bed playing with her dolls.

'I want to cut Molly's hair, but Mummy won't let me.'

Alice looked at the doll's long blonde locks.

'If you cut it, it won't grow back,' she warned.

Cassie gave a patient sigh. 'I know that, Aunty Alice, but I need to practise.'

'You want to be a hairdresser?' Alice thought of the meagre amount Lauren earned. 'There are lots of other things you could do when you leave school.'

'No there aren't. I'm going to have lots of children, so I need to work at home, like Mummy.'

There was no way she could argue with that, Alice decided, awed by the wisdom of her five-year-old niece.

'I'll run your bath and then you can get dressed and come to the library with me. I have to return some money I borrowed from a famous writer.'

'Mummy says you should never borrow things,' Cassie answered primly.

Alice agreed wholeheartedly — but as she'd already committed the sin, all she could now do was try and put it right.

2

How do you make a special effort to impress someone without them knowing? Alice wondered. She wore the minimum amount of make-up when she was teaching her class of pre-teens. Mothers were wary of glamorous teachers, not only because they were trying to protect their children, but because they sometimes sent their husband to pick a child up from school. Short skirts were out, and high necklines were a good idea for a similar reason. She usually scraped her hair back into a ponytail to keep it away from chewing gum and Blu-Tack, and wore flat shoes so that she was less likely to trip over things left lying about on the floor.

But today was different. Her hair was freshly washed and loose on her shoulders and her skirt barely skimmed her knees. Cassie danced beside her, eager to choose a new book for bedtime reading, and Alice felt an odd fluttering in her stomach.

This was silly, she told herself, as she pushed open the double doors into the library. Leo Grant just wanted his money back. Nothing more. This was not a secret tryst. He had probably forgotten about her already.

Although ... maybe not. She had been nothing if not memorable. Who could possibly forget a pink hat with ear flaps teamed with bunny rabbit pyjamas?

Feeling less confident by the minute, she took Cassie's hand and guided her to the children's section where big tubs of books stood between brightly coloured plastic cubes.

'Find a nice book and sit down while I go and give the man his money.' She had spotted Leo talking to the chief librarian. 'I'll be just over there.'

The librarian looked up as she approached. 'Hello, Alice, do you want to order something special?'

Alice shook her head, knowing it made her hair swing. For some reason, she was so short of breath she wasn't sure if she could speak. Leo Grant was looking at her with amusement in his eyes, waiting to hear what she was going to say.

'No thanks, Caroline. I came to see Mr Grant. He was kind enough to help me out at the supermarket last night. I left home without any money.' She took a twenty-pound note out of her purse and held it out to Leo. 'I'm very grateful.'

'My pleasure.'

He took the note slowly, trailing the tips of his fingers down the palm of her hand, and she felt her toes curl.

'Actually, Alice might be just the person you're looking for,' Caroline said. 'She teaches at the local school and she has a degree in English. I'm sure she'd be only too pleased to edit your book.'

'Oh, I've never done any editing,'

Alice said quickly. She had a vision of marking Leo's book like an exam paper, covering it with comments in red ink. She didn't think he'd take kindly to that. 'I'd have no idea where to start.'

'The beginning might be a good place. I don't need someone to re-write the book — just check for typos and things like that.'

He looked past her and dropped into a crouch. 'Hello sweetheart, where did you come from?'

'Over there,' Cassie said, taking the question literally. 'I've chosen a book, Aunty Alice.'

Leo took the book gently out of Cassie's hands. 'It's about a hungry caterpillar. Can you read it by yourself?'

'I might need a little help. Some of the words are long.'

'Yes, they are, aren't they? I don't think I can read all of them.' He flicked through the pages. 'I think I might need a little help as well.'

'Mr Grant writes books,' the librarian offered helpfully.

Cassie looked at the man squatting in front of her with renewed interest. 'Did you write this book?'

'No. I'm not clever enough to write a book like that.'

'Does your book have a dragon in it? And a prince and princess?' Cassie's eyes sparkled.

'Well — it kinda does. It has a handsome man and a pretty lady in it — but no dragon, I'm afraid. Perhaps you can read one of my books when you're a bit older.' He got to his feet and held out his hand to Cassie who shook it solemnly.

'Can we go now?' she asked Alice.

'Yes, of course we can. Let's go and check the caterpillar book out with your library card and then we'll go.' She looked up at Leo Grant. 'I'm sorry. She's always in a hurry.'

'How about my book? It still needs editing and the schools are out so you're not working at the moment. I pay real well.'

His accent was beginning to annoy

her. He had been born in England, after all.

'I have an enormous amount of work to get through, and just because I didn't have any money last night doesn't mean I'm desperate.' Belatedly Alice realised how rude she sounded and tried to backtrack. 'Thank you again for coming to my rescue, Mr Grant, but even though the schools are off for the holiday, I have a lot of work to do. I'll be in and out of here, I expect,' she told Caroline. 'It's difficult to work from home with Cassie around all day but Lauren needs me to babysit some of the time.'

'I'm not a baby,' Cassie complained, as Alice grabbed her by the hand and hurried her out of the library. 'And I only need to hold hands to cross the road.'

'Fine. Here's a road to cross, so you need to hold my hand.'

'Why are you angry, Aunty Alice?'

Alice slowed down and took a breath. 'I'm not angry, sweetheart — not with you, anyway. Shall we go and buy you a cake in the cake shop? Mummy might like one, too.'

Pacified, Cassie chose three cupcakes and carried the bag carefully out of the shop.

'That man at the library was nice. He had pretty hair.'

'Yes, he did, didn't he?'

Alice had the colour of Leo's hair emblazoned on her heart. It had not been a good idea to see him again. He was even more gorgeous second time around — and just as far out of reach.

The possessive way the redhead had been hanging on to his arm in the supermarket left no doubt where he belonged. Alice knew she scrubbed up pretty well, but she also knew her limitations, and Leo Grant was definitely way out of her reach.

The cakes were greeted with enthusiasm and a fresh pot of tea. Cassie asked for permission to play her computer game and took the remains of her cake upstairs with her. She had already carefully eaten all the chocolate frosting off the top, but was saving the sponge part for later, she told them happily.

Once they were alone, Alice looked worriedly at her sister. Lauren was white-faced and looked as if she might have been crying. 'What's up?'

'The car insurance renewal arrived. It's gone up by over two hundred pounds. Even if we pay it monthly, it's going to leave us really short.' She bit her lip. 'It's that prang I had, isn't it?'

'Probably, but there's nothing we can do about that. I'll look online and see if I can get the insurance cheaper somewhere else.' Alice didn't hold out much hope. Her sister had reversed the car out of a parking space just as another car was driving past. Both vehicles had been badly damaged and they had already paid the two-hundred-pound excess on the insurance.

'Nobody was hurt, that was the main thing, and the car's been repaired, so we've still got something to drive.'

'Could we do without the car?' Lauren asked hopefully. 'You get a bus most mornings, and I can walk Cassie to school.'

They might have to get rid of the car at some point in the future, but public transport couldn't always take Alice where she wanted to go and, for the moment, she could manage the extra insurance money.

'We'll see how we go.' She smiled reassuringly.

'The boiler's packed up again, as well,' Lauren said apologetically. 'I thought I'd better get all the bad news over at once, then we can enjoy the rest of the day.'

The boiler was more of a worry than the car — a new boiler would cost at least a couple of thousand pounds — but Alice had managed to get it going again last time it stopped, so she could probably do so again.

Their mother had always told them both not to worry about things that might not happen — but some of the impending disasters seemed pretty inevitable.

'You've got another client in half an hour, so I'll take the rest of my work upstairs to Cassie's room. She won't bother me if she's on her little computer.'

'How did you get on with Mr Wonderful? I was going to ask, but then I got sidetracked with bills and things.'

'Cassie thinks he has pretty hair and he offered me a job — said he pays well, apparently,' Alice said, rolling her eyes.

'Doing what?' Lauren asked, immediately suspicious.

'Don't worry. He wants someone to edit his manuscript, that's all, but I know nothing whatsoever about editing.'

'It's just marking, isn't it? Like you do with the kids' papers. And how much does 'pays well' mean?'

'I don't know. I didn't ask. I can't do it, Lauren, I have my own work to do and you need me to look after Cassie.

You can't let her run loose while you're colouring someone's hair.'

'No, I suppose not,' Lauren agreed reluctantly. 'But we could do with the extra money.'

Alice took the last bite of cake. 'I'll go and fix the boiler.'

She managed to get the boiler going again by turning it off at the mains and giving it a good bang with her fist before she turned it on again. They now had heat and hot water for a while longer, but she knew it couldn't go on.

She phoned the local boiler repair service and asked them to come out, but she knew what they'd say. The boiler was so old, it was getting dangerous — and they had a child in the house.

She climbed into bed that night wondering what it would be like to work for Leo Grant.

*   *   *

The next day she took Cassie to the park while Lauren cut and coloured a client's hair. She had to be back by lunchtime because the man was coming to give them an estimate for the boiler, but for the moment she was enjoying the sun and trying not to think about what would happen if the boiler couldn't be repaired. A jug of hot water was no longer considered adequate equipment for a hairstylist.

Cassie gave up her tour of the various climbing frames and flopped on to the bench next to Alice.

'Is the library man your boyfriend?'

'Whatever made you ask that?' Alice said, startled. 'I hardly know him.'

'Oh.' Cassie pulled a disappointed face. 'I like him. He's nice. I didn't like Jason.'

Jason had been last year. Another tall blond, but with freckles and slightly buck teeth — and definitely no pretty hair. Jason's hair — and personality, come to that — had been reminiscent of a damp straw bale.

'Why do you like Leo Grant?' Alice asked curiously. The child had only spoken to him for a second or two.

'I told you. Because he's got golden hair and blue eyes, like a prince. I'm going on the slide now.' With that the little girl skipped away again.

Reason enough, probably, Alice thought with a smile. She gave Cassie another five minutes and then collected her niece from the play area. 'We have to go home now. Mummy will have finished with her lady and we've got tomato soup for lunch.'

'Can we get more chocolate cupcakes to have afterwards?'

'I don't see why not.'

The boiler was evidently in its death throes. Six months maximum, but total failure could happen as soon as next week. A new boiler could be ordered straight away and payment could be made in instalments.

'We can't,' Lauren whispered. 'You pay enough already, Alice. I can't expect you to contribute any more.' She twisted her hands together. 'I suppose if we're lucky, it might last for another six months.'

31

'And it might not. It will be cold by then and you can't work without heat and hot water. We don't have any choice.' Alice took hold of her sister's hands. 'I'll do Leo Grant's editing for him. I can work from home and still keep an eye on Cassie for you. Incidentally, she thinks he has pretty hair.'

'Send him to me if he needs a haircut, then! He might as well pay both of us while he's at it. Seriously though, Alice, will you be okay? You said you know nothing about editing.'

'I don't, but how hard can it be? It's a contemporary thriller, not a literary work, and Leo Grant said it's only checking spelling errors and things like that. I have to do things like that already, don't I? I'll be just fine.'

She didn't feel fine as she picked up the phone. She had no idea what Leo Grant's telephone number was or where he was staying, so she phoned Caroline at the library.

'Yes, I've got his number. He's

staying with his father in the village. I'm so glad you changed your mind about helping him with his editing. He seems a really nice man. Charming and good-looking. You should have fun.'

Alice had a vision of a tall redhead with a body to kill for. *She* was the one having all the fun!

Before her courage deserted her completely, Alice dialled the number she had written down.

A woman answered and Alice almost put the phone back in its cradle, but the voice sounded older and the woman had a strong Mediterranean accent. Definitely not the redhead.

'May I speak to Mr Leo Grant, please? My name is Alice Prescott.' By the time he came on the line her hand had just about stopped shaking.

'Hi, Alice. What can I do for you? Gone shopping without your wallet again?'

If she hadn't needed the job she would have hung up.

'I called about the editing job. Is it still available?'

It hadn't crossed her mind until then, but if he was in a hurry he might have already found someone else.

'It might be. Are you offering your services?'

She wouldn't have put it quite like that. 'If you think I'd be of help. Exactly what does editing a manuscript entail?'

'Come on over and we'll discuss it. Nothing difficult, but it's hard to explain over the phone.'

Not today; it would be dinnertime soon and Lauren might need help. 'I can come to see you in the morning, if you like. What's the address?' He gave directions to a street on the other side of the village. 'I'll find it.'

'See you tomorrow, then. Can you make it about ten? I'm not an early riser.'

Alice put the phone down. Now what had she managed to get herself into? She sighed. She had to remind herself that the money was more important than her feelings — and she had no idea what she was feeling. Trepidation was a good word.

'I'm going to see him tomorrow morning,' she told Lauren.

'So you've got the job. Brilliant!'

'It's not definite, and there's no point in doing it at all unless the money's good. I still have some marking to do for the school that I can't put on hold.'

'But you'll get to spend time with Leo Grant, and even Cassie seems quite smitten. I'm going to have to meet him sometime.'

'He's a bit . . . I don't know, really. He's pretty sure of himself, and he seems to find me amusing — which is quite irritating.'

'I'd find you amusing if I'd seen you at the supermarket in your nightclothes. I still don't know what possessed you to go out in your pyjamas.'

'Lots of people do,' Alice said defensively. 'In a dressing gown and slippers, sometimes. At least I took the trouble to put on a jacket and boots.'

'And Cassie's little pink woolly hat,' Lauren reminded her with a giggle.

35

Alice decided to change the subject. 'Leo Grant is staying on the other side of the village near the river. I don't recognise the road name but he's staying with his father. If the man's a surgeon it's probably quite a big house. Surgeons get paid a lot of money, don't they?'

She wondered whether the redhead girlfriend was staying at the house as well. 'Do you think he brought that redhead over from America with him? She looks sort of American — and you should see her hair. You'd probably know what she uses to get it that colour.'

Lauren grinned. 'Meow! I'll see if I can find out. Not what hair colour she uses — but whether she's American. One of my customers will know. Between them they know everything that goes on in the village.'

Cassie was tired, and Lauren sent her up to bed soon after dinner. Alice waited until her niece had been bathed and tucked up in bed and then went upstairs to read the usual bedtime story. Cassie nearly always chose the same book, a variation on *Sleeping Beauty*, and Alice knew the story off by heart. A prince with golden hair, riding a white horse, rescuing a princess.

Cassie was yawning by the time the story was finished.

'Mummy says you're going to see that nice man tomorrow,' the little girl said sleepily, snuggling down under her duvet. 'Will you give him a kiss for me?'

Alice was desperately trying to put all thoughts of Leo Grant — and kisses — out of her mind as she sat down on the sofa beside her sister.

Lauren held out a card-mounted print. 'Look what I found! A school photo. See? I told you he had spots, but I'd forgotten about the glasses.'

Alice stared at the photo and Leo Grant stared back. He was in the back row, possibly because of his height, and he looked startled, as if the flash of the camera had caught him by surprise. He did have spots, and those bright, intelligent eyes were hidden behind dark-rimmed glasses, but even at eleven or twelve he was still a head taller than his classmates. His hair was too long even then, thick and unruly, the colour an even brown with no hint of the golden highlights to come.

Alice smiled. She wasn't feeling nearly so apprehensive about tomorrow. The school photo had done away with all Leo Grant's celebrity status and deposited him firmly back among the ordinary people.

Tomorrow would be pure business, and she would dress in keeping with her occupation. Leo Grant had seen her looking like a bag lady, and then done up in her Sunday best; now he was about to meet the English teacher.

Before she went to bed, she laid out a smart navy skirt and demure white blouse. Depending on the weather, she would wear a matching jacket or a navy cardigan. She decided to indulge herself with a pair of strappy, high-heeled sandals that showed off her legs.

She didn't want Leo Grant to forget that she was a girl.

3

Alice found the house she was looking for at the end of a short, unmade road. The building was a rectangle of old, red brick covered with ivy, tall chimneys thrusting into the sky, leaded windows, and a heavy oak front door.

There was no bell push to be seen, so she swung the knocker and listened to the sound reverberate through the building. It was some minutes before she heard footsteps and the door was opened — not by Leo Grant, but by an equally tall man with cool grey eyes and a surprised expression.

'Yes?'

'I'm sorry. I think I must have made a mistake. I'm looking for Leo Grant, the author.'

'Is that what he calls himself now? 'Leo Grant, the author'? Perhaps I should rename myself Peter Grant, the surgeon.'

Alice smiled with relief. 'I'm Alice Prescott and you must be Leo's father. I should have realised. He's very like you.'

'Apart from a rather considerable age difference. But I'll take that as a compliment. Please come in.'

In the middle of the parquet-floored hall Peter Grant stopped suddenly and Alice nearly ran into him. 'Tiffany, there's someone here to see Leo.'

With a sinking feeling, Alice heard someone descending the stairs and looked up. The redhead was coming down the long flight slowly, holding on to the banister rail. Her denim skirt stopped mid-thigh, emphasising long, smooth, golden legs. Her bright red hair was loose round her shoulders and the smattering of freckles across the bridge of her nose did nothing to detract from a perfect oval face. She would have looked equally good, Alice decided, in bunny pyjamas and a pink woolly hat.

The doctor waited until the vision reached the bottom of the stairs. 'Take Miss Prescott to the library, please,

Tiffany. Leo's locked himself away again.'

'He's working.' Tiffany bent forward elegantly and peered at Alice through designer spectacles with dark, brown-tinted lenses. 'Are you the girl from the supermarket?' she asked.

Alice's face went pink. She had hoped Tiffany wouldn't recognise her. 'The one with no money? Yes I am, unfortunately. I did thank Leo and repay him the money he lent me.'

'Not a problem, but it must have been so embarrassing for you at the time.'

You don't know the half of it, Alice thought, as Tiffany pushed open a door into a room packed from floor to ceiling with shelves of books. A quick glance told her that the books were mostly a mixture of medical journals and popular fiction, a rolling ladder giving access to the upper shelves where older-looking volumes leaned against one another.

A large desk made of highly polished

walnut was covered almost completely with pages of manuscript, scattered randomly, and Alice's fingers itched to restore some sort of order. She had never been able to work in a mess. A laptop sat perched on top of the pages, the screen filled with text.

Leo looked up, at first annoyed at the interruption, but then his face broke into a smile. 'Well, well, my two favourite girls. This must be my lucky day.'

Tiffany pulled a face. 'Watch him,' she told Alice. 'He's full of phoney charm, just like his novels.'

As she left the room, Leo pushed the door closed behind her. 'There's not enough room in here. I have twice this space at home, but it can't be helped.'

Alice looked around helplessly. 'You'd have more room if you kept things tidy. How do you manage to work like this?'

'Just fine, thank you, I don't need a lecture on tidiness.' He said the words lightly, but his voice had an edge of annoyance. 'My editor suggested dealing with the changes to the manuscript online, but that doesn't work for me.'

'Can I take the manuscript home? That would be easier.'

He looked at her, scandalised, as if she had suggested wearing the crown jewels to shop at Tesco.

'I don't think so. I don't let this version out of my sight, ever.'

'But you've got it on your hard drive. You can print as many copies as you like.'

'But I can only edit one copy at a time, and that copy stays right here with me. If you can't spare the time to come over here each day, we'll have to think again.'

'How much are you paying?' she asked bluntly. She'd need a lot of money to drop everything and leave her sister in the lurch during the school holidays.

He mentioned an amount that left Alice slightly breathless.

'You can shuffle the time you spend here to suit yourself, within reason,' he went on. 'Say about four hours a day if you can manage that? I've got a little over a month before the final edit is due back with the publisher. I'll still have the proof copy to go through, but I'll be back home by then.'

'If I do this, how long will you need me?'

'It depends how well we work together. About three or four weeks, I guess. After that I'll be pushing the deadline.'

Alice did a bit of mental arithmetic. That would pay for the boiler twice over.

'I might have to look after Cassie some of the time. Perhaps I could do more hours some days and fewer on others.'

Leo shook his head. 'I don't work more than four hours a day when I'm editing a book. Sometimes I'm up all night when I'm writing the damn thing, but that's the fun part. Once that's done, I go part-time. Besides,' he grinned at her, 'I live in LA. No one there works any longer than they have to.'

'I'll talk to my sister. She's a hairdresser, but she works from home, and I help with Cassie when I can.'

'Of course. You're a teacher, so you're home during the school holidays. It sounds like a perfect arrangement.'

'It usually is.'

'Tell you what — bring the little girl with you. We've got an enormous garden and Grace will love to look after her.'

'Grace?' How many women did this man have?

'My father's housekeeper. She's about sixty, she loves kids, and she's been with us for years. Ever since I was born, I think. I'll introduce you later on and you can see what you think.' He picked up a sheet of manuscript seemingly at random and handed it to her. 'See what you make of this.'

Alice quickly scanned the page. 'Some speech marks missing. A comma when you should have used a semi-colon.' She handed it back to him. 'And a bit of an information dump in paragraph four. I don't need to know how many bullets a Sig Sauer Glock fires.'

'Yes, you do. Later on the guy runs out of bullets in a gun fight.' He sighed. 'I was afraid of this. We need to get something straight right from the off. I just want a punctuation and grammar check. I'm quite capable of doing the writing all on my own, that's why I get paid such an obscene sum of money for each book I write.'

He didn't frown or raise his voice, she noticed. He just spoke slowly and quietly as if she had the mentality of a goldfish.

If she lost her temper, she would probably lose the job as well. *Button your lip, Alice,* her mother used to say.

'I think I can manage that,' she said evenly. 'I do have a degree in English language.'

'Good for you.' He pulled all the pages together and shuffled them into a reasonably tidy heap. Then he closed the laptop and lined it up exactly with the edge of the desk. 'That should meet your tidiness requirements. Can you start tomorrow?'

When she nodded, he opened the door into the hall and followed her out.

'Come and let me introduce you to Grace. You can decide if Cassie will be safe with her.'

He led the way across the hall and down a short passage that led to the kitchen; an enormous room with a wooden floor and modern kitchen units in pale wood. A stainless steel range looked as if it meant business, and pans of every size and shape hung from a rack over an island unit.

A large lady in a very white apron, her black hair twisted into a bun, was stirring a pot on the stove. Alice thought she could smell tomato soup, home-made with a hint of basil and some other herb she couldn't identify.

'Grace, this is Alice. She'll be working with me for a few weeks on the book, and sometimes she may bring her niece with her. Can you keep the kiddie amused for a few hours?'

Grace looked up from her pot. 'How old?'

Leo grinned. 'Ah — I remember, Grace doesn't like changing diapers. Don't worry, this one's fine. She's school age.'

'Cassie's five,' Alice said. 'She's just started a reception class at the local junior school, but she's home now because of the holidays.'

'Five is nice,' Grace said, her attention back with her pot. 'And a girl. That's good. Boys run and I'm too fat to chase.'

'You weren't at one time,' Leo said with a laugh. 'You chased me all over the place when I was a kid, usually to spank my backside.' He turned to Alice. 'I'll show you the back yard. As far as I can remember, it's safe enough.'

The garden was huge, with lots of trees and flower borders, and a little path leading to an orchard. There was no sign of a pond or other water feature and Alice was glad about that, but she still wasn't entirely happy about leaving

49

Cassie in the care of a stranger.

'I'll have to check with my sister, but if she agrees I'll be here tomorrow at ten.' She looked at him curiously. 'You could just do a grammar and spell check on the computer, you know. Why do you need me?'

He waved a hand dismissively. 'A computer spell check isn't the same. It might be fine for a business document, but this is fiction. It doesn't work.'

Alice bit her tongue and thought of the boiler. She really needed this job, but it might prove harder than she thought if he was going to use American spelling and muck about with the English language to suit his whim.

He led her back through the house and into the living room, where his father was reading a book. The older man looked up with a frown.

'Tiffany is wandering around somewhere on her own, Leo. Someone needs to keep an eye on that girl.'

'Tiffany's not a child, Dad, and I'm not her keeper. She'll be just fine.'

'If you say so, but I'll be at the hospital all day tomorrow.'

Leo smiled at Alice and rolled his eyes. 'I'll see Alice out and then I'll find Tiffany. Don't worry, she won't have gone far.'

'I hope not,' Dr Grant said without looking up from his book.

'Tiffany came with you from America, did she?' Alice asked curiously as Leo opened the front door. She could understand Leo fussing over the girl, but his father seemed just as concerned. And from what she had seen, Tiffany was quite capable of looking after herself.

'Yes, she did.'

When he didn't say anything else Alice walked with him across the gravel drive and climbed into her car. 'I'll see you tomorrow, then.'

He gave her an enigmatic smile and slammed the car door.

★ ★ ★

51

Alice drove home with more questions than when she had arrived. Tiffany was beautiful, but much younger than she had originally thought. She had only had a brief glimpse of the girl in the supermarket, but on closer inspection Tiffany couldn't be a day over eighteen.

Alice had never been the brightest star in the firmament as far as maths was concerned, but if Leo was in the same class as Lauren at school, he must be roughly the same age. She shrugged. None of her business.

But the first thing she did when she arrived home was question her sister.

'Leo Grant is the same age as you, isn't he?'

'Yes, he must be if we were in the same class. Thirty-one sometime this year.' Lauren pulled a face. 'Don't rub my nose in it, please.'

'I don't reckon the girlfriend is much over eighteen.'

Lauren grinned. 'I wouldn't have thought that was your problem, but I have a bit more news for you, as it happens. She's not his girlfriend; she's his sister — or rather, half-sister, actually. Mummy obviously didn't waste any time when she landed in America.'

Alice felt one of those little twists in reality that happen now and again. She had found it quite easy to keep her distance from Leo while he had a girlfriend — she would never encroach on someone else's territory — but this changed things in a subtle way she couldn't quite put her finger on.

'Are you sure?'

Lauren wiggled her eyebrows. 'Ah yes. My informant is to be completely trusted.'

'I suppose I should have guessed. Leo doesn't come across as a baby snatcher, although he's quite protective of her. I met Dr Grant at the house, too, and he seemed to be really worried about losing sight of her. Almost as if she's not safe to be out on her own.'

Alice wondered if this was the first time Dr Grant had met Tiffany. If this was the girl's first visit to England, it might perhaps explain his anxiety, but he had seemed to treat her as if she wasn't quite right in the head.

'More importantly,' Lauren asked, 'did you get the job?'

'Yes, but I have to go to the house each day. He says I can take Cassie with me if I need to. The doctor has an elderly housekeeper who'll keep an eye on her and I won't be far away.'

'I suppose that should be okay. Cassie has a real thing going for Leo Grant, so she'll be happy to go with you. She thinks he's a prince in disguise.'

Alice snorted. 'Well, I've already met the princess. His baby sister is absolutely gorgeous, besides being very young.'

'You're only twenty-five, Alice. I wish I was your age again.'

As Lauren went to prepare Cassie a sandwich for lunch, Alice sighed. Five years ago, Lauren had been pregnant with Cassie and her husband had still been alive. Their mother had been alive then, too.

Alice couldn't believe so much had happened in five years. The only really good thing to come out of it all had been Cassie — even though the little girl's daddy had been killed just before she was born.

Not one to dwell on the past, Alice gave herself a mental shake and went to help her sister in the kitchen.

★   ★   ★

'What's the house like?' Lauren asked, as she thawed slices of bread in the microwave.

'The house is lovely, an old ivy-covered building. The garden is huge with little paths and lots of trees — but not a pond in sight, you'll be happy to know, so Cassie will be quite safe. You mentioned that Leo's father is a surgeon, didn't you?'

'Yes. He works in London some-where. No one has seen Leo Grant's sister yet, but someone has told someone else that she's a model.'

'Hmm. That figures, given her height and looks.'

'I wonder why Leo brought her back to England with him? Come to think of it, why did *he* come back? Was it to introduce Daddy to his stepdaughter, do you think?'

'I don't know.' Alice frowned. 'Leo doesn't like being questioned. He's got this little smile he uses, as if the question is really stupid, so you don't ask anything else. Not like your gossipy ladies who obviously like answering questions. What else did you learn?'

'Lots about Daddy but not much about the son or daughter. In America, Leo is just beginning to get noticed as a promising author. He's put a twist on the thriller by having a female as his new action hero. Similar to Lara Croft, I would imagine. Every man's dream and every woman's aspiration.'

'Not my cup of tea.' Alice buttered enough bread for all three of them. 'But

I'm going to have to read his latest book while I'm editing it, aren't I? Leo said spelling and grammar aren't the same for fiction, and he could be right, so I'll have to be careful. He told me quite specifically that it's not my job to rewrite his book for him.'

'So take his advice and don't try. Don't alter anything without checking with him first, will you?' Lauren said worriedly. 'I know what you're like when it comes to your precious English language — and he's right, fiction is different. In a novel you can start a sentence with 'And'.'

Alice threw up her hands in mock horror. 'Heaven forbid!'

Her sister laughed. 'You're going to have to make sacrifices for the sake of us all. How long will you have to work for him?'

'No more than four weeks, and I'll make enough to pay for our new boiler with some over.'

'Wow! Really? Do you have to sleep with him?'

'I wish.' Alice grinned. 'Now I know he's free . . . '

'Yeah.' Lauren sighed. 'Pity I'm a poor single parent. Otherwise I might have stood a chance myself.' She laughed.

'Oi!' Alice retorted, jokingly. 'In your dreams, girl! Back off — I saw him first!'

Cassie came into the kitchen holding a headless doll. 'She's lost her head again, Mummy.'

'So have we,' Lauren said with a giggle. 'Aunty Alice is going to work for Leo Grant, that man you like, and you may have to go with her sometimes. Is that okay with you?'

'Yes!' Cassie danced around. 'Does he live in a castle?'

'Not quite.' Alice bent down in front of her niece. 'He lives in a big house with a big garden, but I'll be close by all the time, so you can come and find me if you need me.'

'I won't,' Cassie announced. 'I'm at big school now, so I'm all grown up.'

'Not quite, young lady.' Lauren pulled out a chair and waited for Cassie to climb up. 'Eat your sandwich.'

Cassie lifted the top slice of bread and surveyed the contents. 'What is it?'

'Corned beef.'

'Is that meat?' Cassie asked suspiciously.

'You saw me open the can. Meat doesn't come out of a can, does it?'

'No, it comes from an animal, like a cow or a dog, and I don't like it.'

'That is not dog, I promise you. I absolutely guarantee there is no dog in that sandwich, so stop arguing and eat your food like someone who goes to big school.'

'Can I have a caterpillar to go with it?'

Lauren forked a small green gherkin out of the pickle jar and put it on Cassie's plate. 'One caterpillar coming up.'

Alice shook her head sadly. 'That child is going to grow up to be really strange.'

4

Grace opened the front door with a frown and peered over Alice's shoulder. 'Where is the child I am to look after?'

'I didn't bring Cassie this morning,' Alice answered. The woman was filling the doorway like a barricade. 'Her mother can manage her today.'

Grace grunted and moved aside to let Alice into the hallway. 'What's she do that she can't look after her own daughter?'

'She works for a living,' Alice answered, a touch frostily. She was nervous enough already without having to go through an interrogation from the housekeeper. 'I just help her out in the school holidays.'

The woman gave another grunt as she led the way across the hall and opened the library door. 'Wait here. Mister Leo will come soon.' She shut the door as she went out and Alice found herself alone.

The desk was now reasonably tidy, the manuscript in a neat pile and the laptop closed — so he had made an effort. A stand-alone hard drive and a couple of flash drives lay in a plastic tray and she wondered how many copies he made of everything.

The man was obviously paranoid about his novel, but that wasn't her problem, and she must remember not to question his use of the English language. He had been living in America for quite a while after all. Fine; she could handle that. But commas and full stops were the same in any language, although — she smiled wryly — come to think of it, he would probably call a full stop a period.

The room seemed well used. A couple of rugs covered most of the wood floor and a worn, button-back Chesterfield looked comfortable enough to sleep on. A real fire was set, ready to light, and Alice could imagine herself sprawling on the sofa in front of the fire with a good book. A snowy winter evening would be a positive pleasure in a room like this, she thought.

It was nice of the doctor to give up what was obviously a very personal place to his son; but it was only for a month, and then Leo and his sister would go home to America and the doctor would have the place to himself again. Would that please him? she wondered. The house seemed too big for a single man with only a grumpy housekeeper to keep him company.

Leo opened the door quietly and stood watching her until she sensed his presence and turned round. He smiled, closing the door behind him, and Alice wondered why she felt so nervous in his presence. Tiffany was nowhere in sight, but Grace was around somewhere. It wasn't as if she was alone in the house with the man. It just felt that way.

'Hi,' he said softly, running his eyes over her in a way that had her blushing.

Had she overdone the efficient look?

She smoothed her skirt and wished he'd look somewhere else. 'Good morning. Where do you want to start?'

He smiled. 'My day usually starts with coffee, so that's where we'll begin. See,' he waved a hand, 'I can be tidy when I try, but I don't promise it will stay that way.' His smile widened. 'You look as nervous as a kitten, Alice. Contrary to village gossip, I don't actually bite.'

At that moment Grace pushed the door open and backed into the room holding a tray. Without a word, she set the tray down on a small table and left.

Alice looked at the cafetière. 'Do you want me to be mum?'

When he looked puzzled, she explained the idiom. 'Shall I pour out the coffee?'

'Ah. Yes, please.'

He watched her in a way she found unnerving. It was as if he was taking a mental picture and filing it away for future reference. She hoped she didn't turn up in one of his books.

'Where's your sister this morning?' she asked, handing him a glass mug of coffee, slightly disappointed when he didn't look surprised.

'Tiffany? Probably still in bed.' He added cream from a tiny jug and stirred in two spoons of sugar. 'It didn't take long for you to discover that she's my sister. Who was your source of information?'

Alice put cream in her own coffee but waved away the sugar. 'A good spy never gives away her source,' she said lightly.

'Ah,' he said again, this time with a cool smile. 'I remember now. Your sister has a hair salon. I'm sure there is plenty of gossip going around. What else did she manage to discover about my family?'

'Don't flatter yourself, Mr Grant. No one is that interested in your family's affairs.' *Always think before you speak* was another piece of advice she should have heeded. She wished she had chosen her words with more care, but she couldn't take them back. 'The fact that you have a half-sister seems to be common knowledge.'

'Good. That saves me having to explain to everyone.' He put his mug down carefully on the polished desk. 'Some people might have thought she was my girlfriend.'

'Surely not.' Alice hoped she wasn't blushing again. 'Tiffany is a bit young, even for you.'

'I'm not sure what that means, exactly, but perhaps we'd better get to work before you fall into that hole you're digging.'

⋆ ⋆ ⋆

The morning passed swiftly for Alice. She was learning as she went along. Leo insisted on keeping all the contractions, even in the descriptive passages, and frequently used commas in places that made her shudder, but she kept her mouth shut and he seemed happy with what she was doing.

'Finish the first chapter on your own, and then I'll have a look to see if I agree with what you've done.' He looked at the gold watch nestling amongst the pale hairs on his wrist. 'After that, I think we'll stop for lunch.'

'Oh, I don't expect you to feed me,' Alice said immediately.

He raised an eyebrow. 'I need to eat at certain times of the day, and Grace will provide enough food for both of us, but I had no intention of feeding you.'

She was never sure whether he was being serious or not, so she just smiled politely. 'Fair enough. I'm sure I can manage to feed myself, thank you.'

The windows in the library were small, and Alice was surprised to walk into the living room and find the doors open on to the terrace, sunlight flooding into the room. Grace had set a buffet lunch outside on the patio; plates of salad and cold meat, warm bread rolls and a jug of what looked like fruit punch. Suddenly hungry, she sat where Leo indicated and helped herself to cold chicken and salad. He filled her glass, spooning in fruit.

'Sangria,' he said. 'I got a taste for it in Spain a couple of years ago.'

Alice slipped off her navy cardigan and let the sun warm her bare arms, wishing she had dressed more casually. Her tights were itching and her skirt was tight round her waist. Bunny pyjamas would have been more comfortable.

She must have smiled because he raised a quizzical eyebrow. 'What are you thinking about?'

'I was thinking I'm overdressed.'

She was getting used to the slow smile that tipped the corner of his mouth and creased the skin beside his eyes. 'If nightwear would be more comfortable, please feel free. We have no particular dress code round here.'

The man could obviously read her mind. She knew she had to be careful what she said out loud, but she couldn't always guard her thoughts. 'Bunny pyjamas? I don't think so. Not in front of your beautiful sister, anyway. I know I can't compete, but I won't surrender without a fight. I have my pride.'

'I could tell that by your choice of hat the other night. The pink knitted number was inspired.'

She grinned back at him. 'I thought so, too.'

'That reminds me,' he looked at his watch again, 'I'm going to have to wake Tiffany. We've been here a week now and she still hasn't got used to the time difference. She worked in Milan for a while and she said someone always had to drag her out of bed in the morning.' He pushed back his chair. 'I'll ask Grace for more coffee — a shot of caffeine into Tiffany's veins might help. Besides, she needs to eat regularly.'

He was gone before Alice could ask any questions, but she still found it odd that the two men should feel they had to look after Tiffany with such determination, even down to making sure she ate on time. If the girl had been to Milan on her own, it proved she was more than capable of looking after herself, but perhaps Leo had always been made to feel responsible for his little sister. It must have been quite a blow for a young boy to be uprooted from his friends in England and then have a baby arrive a short time later.

Leo came back carrying a full, fragrantly steaming cafetière and refilled their mugs. 'Tiffany will be down in a few minutes.'

'How's she getting on in England? From what you say, she's quite well-travelled.'

'Not really. She's been to Milan, but she prefers California. That's where her home is.'

'And her family and friends. She must feel lonely here without anyone her own age. I'd be happy to take her to the shopping centre next time I go, if she'd like to look around.'

Alice couldn't imagine what had possessed her. It would be positively humiliating to go shopping with someone like Tiffany and, besides, there would be nothing at Breakwater Shopping Centre to rival Milan or Paris.

She was quite relieved when Leo dismissed her offer as if he found the concept as ludicrous as she had done in retrospect.

'Thanks for the thought, but Tiffany doesn't go out much, and we won't be staying in England for long.'

He changed the subject before she could come up with any more ridiculous suggestions. 'If you think you can get the first edit done by the end of the week, we can go over it together. Some of the changes you make won't be necessary, but I'll spot those fairly easily, and I'm sure you're familiar with the differences between English and American spelling.'

Before Alice could reply, Tiffany came out on to the terrace wearing a silk robe, her feet bare, her hair a fall of soft red curls. She squinted at the sun and lowered herself onto a chair, pulling it up to the table. 'Morning,' she said with a yawn.

'It's afternoon, actually, Tiffany, and you need to eat.'

'Give it up, Leo,' Tiffany answered irritably. 'Alice will think I'm anorexic. Everyone thinks models are anorexic.' She smiled at Alice. 'I like food, but I prefer sleeping, and this feels like the middle of the night to me. What's the sun doing out?'

'Put your sunglasses on if it bothers you,' Leo said impatiently. 'You'll never get used to local time if you stay in bed half the day.'

Tiffany covered her eyes with outsize sunglasses and gave Alice a half-smile. 'He must be impossible to work with. I don't know how you do it.'

Alice smiled back, a twinkle in her eye. 'It's only my first day. I may not last very long.'

Leo stood up and ruffled his sister's hair. 'Shut up and eat, baby girl, and stop being such a smart-ass. You know it doesn't work with me.'

Alice followed him to the front door. 'Thank you for the food. I may have to bring Cassie with me tomorrow. Are you sure that will be okay?'

'We'll just have to wait and see, won't we? Maybe she can get Tiffany out of bed before lunchtime.'

'Oh, I'm sure she can do that.' Alice felt awkward, standing on the doorstep with Leo. Just for a moment she let her imagination stray and wondered what he would do if she dared to deliver Cassie's kiss.

She was still smiling as she drove home.

The morning hadn't been a complete disaster. Surprisingly, Leo had proved easy to work with and Tiffany was much nicer than she'd expected. Although why the two men fussed round her like they did was still a complete mystery.

★ ★ ★

Leo sighed as he watched Alice drive away. He had enjoyed her company and found himself looking forward to tomorrow. Maybe a child running around the house was what they all needed.

He walked back out on to the patio and saw with satisfaction that Tiffany had filled her plate with food.

'What did you think?' he asked.

'Why? You've never asked my opinion before.' Tiffany lifted her glasses and squinted up at him. 'Or is this one more important than the others?'

'Forget I asked. I should have known you wouldn't give me a straight answer.'

Tiffany leaned back in her chair, a smile on her face. 'So she *is* more important.'

Leo turned and walked into the living room, wondering why he felt so cross and restless. The editing was going well; better than he had anticipated, in fact. Alice was doing very well, considering that she was coping with different spelling and different grammar. That wasn't the problem.

He turned his attention back to his sister, making sure she was still eating, and cursed himself for being a fool. She had managed without him for two years, ever since she had taken up professional modelling, but now things had changed and he seemed to have taken on the role of nursemaid again. Not a duty he enjoyed.

His thoughts went back to Alice, and just for a moment he could visualise her in his recurring dream, alone on the narrow shelf of rock, the dragon's breath heating her skin. Any moment the creature would let forth a jet of fire and she would die.

He always awoke with the memory of her eyes wide with shock and horror as she screamed and pulled against her bonds. Never once had the dream gone beyond that point.

Was he incinerated as well, he wondered, as he sat powerless on his horse? Did it even matter? It was only a dream, after all.

Tiffany came in from the garden and slipped an arm round his waist. 'I'm sorry, Leo. I didn't mean to tease. Little

Alice does matter, doesn't she? Go for it, then. What's stopping you?'

He frowned. 'We'll be leaving here in a few weeks.'

'You don't have to come back with me. It will all be over by then. You won't have to look out for me any more.'

He smiled affectionately at her. 'I'll always look out for you. You're still my baby sister, even if you're nearly as tall as I am. Besides, my work is in Los Angeles. That's my home.'

'No.' Tiffany dropped her arm and turned away from him. 'No — Los Angeles is my home. You were born here, Leo, in England. Your father lives here. You have roots in this country.'

He sighed heavily. 'You've met my father, Tiffany and you could see that he wasn't exactly overjoyed to have me back.'

'He's been very good to me, even though I'm not his flesh and blood. He could easily have said no. He could have turned me away.'

'He likes a challenge — always has. But please don't go wandering off again, because I'll get the blame.'

Tiffany moved to the French doors and stood looking out into the garden. 'This is a lovely house, and I do appreciate what your father is doing for me, but I get so terribly bored being stuck here all day.'

'Alice did offer to take you shopping at the local mall.'

She turned back to him, hope hovering in her eyes. 'What did you tell her?'

He felt like a traitor. 'You can't, Tiffany. You know that. My father would kill me.'

'You could come as well. You could look after me. I won't wander off, I promise. Oh, please, Leo! I so need to get out of this stuffy house.'

Would it be so bad if she went shopping? It was something Tiffany needed to do on a regular basis back home, and she was obviously having withdrawal symptoms.

'We'll see. Don't say anything to my father. We'll have to sneak out when he's at the hospital.' He held up his hand as Tiffany jumped up and down. 'I'm not promising anything.'

She took a deep breath and let it out again, excitement brightening her eyes, some colour in her cheeks for the first time since they landed in England.

'You won't have to worry about me, Leo. I'll do exactly what you tell me and I won't wander off, I promise.' She tried a smile. 'If anything goes wrong, this could be my last chance to shop.'

It was his turn to put his arm round her. He pulled her close and stroked her hair as he had when she was a baby. 'Nothing will go wrong, I trust my father one hundred per cent — but you have to take care of yourself, okay?'

'I don't have to take care of myself, not with you around.' She kissed him on the cheek. 'I'm going up to my room and making a list of things I need to buy.'

He walked to the bottom of the

staircase with her. It was easy to forget she was barely eighteen. Her diabetes was enough of a burden, without the other problems that had been thrust upon her, but all he could do was make sure she took her insulin and ate on a regular basis.

When she first left home, she had been so worried about putting on weight she had nearly killed herself, and Leo had made up his mind that would never happen again. But he couldn't watch over her every minute of every day.

Their mother meant well, but she hadn't been very helpful in the early days, insisting that one piece of chocolate cake couldn't possibly do Tiffany any harm — and that it didn't matter when she took her insulin, as long as she took it.

Leo had found himself responsible for his little sister's well-being, and sometimes her life.

He looked on the noticeboard in the kitchen to find out when his father would next be at the hospital. He was back tonight and working from home for the rest of the week, then he had three days in London.

Leo sighed. He didn't like deceiving his father, and he still had a lot of work to do on his book, but Tiffany was right. She needed something more exciting to do than walking to the village shop with Grace.

He went back into the library and tidied up the desk. Tomorrow should be fun, he thought with a wry smile. Alice was bringing Cassie with her and he didn't imagine she was the sort of child to be seen and not heard. He wondered how his father would cope with a child loose in the house. The experience might provide a bit of excitement for everyone.

5

Cassie was up at the crack of dawn sorting through her wardrobe. 'I need something pretty if I'm going to a castle to meet a prince. I need to look like a princess.'

'It's not a castle,' Alice answered tiredly. She hadn't slept well, with dreams invading her sleep and still hovering at the edge of her vision now that she was awake. 'It's a nice house with a nice garden, that's all.'

Cassie pouted. 'I'm going to pretend it's a castle, then.'

'You do that, then come downstairs and have your breakfast. Mummy's making porridge.'

Another pout. 'I don't like porridge.'

Alice rubbed a hand over her eyes. It was going to be one of those days. She just hoped Grace would be able to cope.

'See you downstairs in five minutes — or you visit the prince in your nightie.'

In the kitchen Lauren looked up from the stove where she was stirring a pot. 'Trouble?'

'Not really. She's looking for a dress fit for a princess; convinced she's going to visit a castle and meet a prince. Nothing out of the ordinary.'

Lauren smiled. 'I wonder what dress she'll choose. It will be something really girly. Shall I put ribbons in her hair?'

Alice was also wearing a dress. A simple button-through in deep blue cotton, dotted with tiny white flowers. She had been thinking of Leo when she took it from its hanger. Perhaps she should put ribbons in *her* hair.

'Whatever makes Cassie happy. Don't worry, I'll keep an eye on her.'

'I know you will.' Lauren stirred the porridge complacently. 'If she's a nuisance, bring her home. I'm sure I can colour hair and watch Cassie at the same time. I just worry about getting side-tracked and turning someone bright orange.'

Alice laughed. 'And we can't afford a lawsuit, not even with the extra money, so I'll worry about Cassie and you worry about hair. We'll see how she gets on today. It will be a good test, because Leo's father and his sister will both be at home.'

At that moment Cassie entered the kitchen and did a rather hesitant twirl. 'Do I look like a princess?' the little girl asked worriedly. 'Or have I overdid it?'

'It's overdone, sweetheart, not over-did, but we know what you mean.' Alice thought Cassie had been quite conservative in her choice of dress. 'You look just wonderful, and that is a perfect princess dress — but put a cardigan on, because otherwise you're going to be cold.'

'And you need a bib if you're going to eat porridge in it,' Lauren added. She took a clean tea towel out of a drawer and draped it round her daughter's neck. 'A princess can't be seen wearing a mucky dress.'

* * *

Alice was still feeling slightly apprehensive twenty minutes later, when she turned in to the drive of the house and parked her car.

'Wow, it *is* a castle,' Cassie commented, looking up. 'It's got things on top.'

Alice didn't bother to point out that the 'things' were tall chimneys and not turrets. Cassie was already in a world of make-believe.

Grace opened the front door with a smile instead of her usual frown. 'You bring the child today.' She bent down in front of Cassie. 'What is your name?'

The little girl faced the big woman fearlessly.

'Cassie. What's yours?'

'You can call me Grace.' She held out her hand and Cassie took it. 'I'll watch her for you,' she told Alice. 'You go and help Mister Leo with his book.'

Realising that she had been dismissed, Alice found her own way to the library and went in without knocking.

Leo looked up from the desk. 'Did you bring Cassie?'

'Yes, she's with Grace. I hope she won't be a nuisance.'

'Grace is great with kids. If she coped with me, she can cope with anyone. We'll stop for lunch a bit earlier so Cassie won't be too hungry. I remember getting really antsy if I needed to eat.'

Alice watched him as he bent over his laptop, his hair catching the light from the window. She could understand why Cassie thought he was a prince.

'There are a few points I need to check with you. Do you want to go over them now?'

He shook his head without looking up. 'I've got Lyra stuck at the bottom of a well and I'm not sure how to get her up. I think the drug baron is going to nail the lid down.'

Alice shook her head in disbelief. 'You must know what's going to happen — you're writing the story.'

Now he looked up, the half-smile she now knew so well tipping the corner of his mouth. 'I never know what's going to happen. That would spoil all my fun. Can you manage on your own here for a bit?'

When Alice nodded, he picked up his laptop and took it out into the garden, leaving Alice on her own.

She had only been working on her editing for about an hour when the door opened and Tiffany poked her head into the room.

'Are you alone? My stepfather's around somewhere and I'm trying to avoid him. He fusses over me all the time.'

'Come in and sit for a minute,' Alice said. 'They both fuss over you, don't they? If I was your age it would drive me insane.'

'They mean well.' Tiffany parked herself on the Chesterfield and crossed her long legs. 'Leo has always looked after me, poor thing. He must have thought he'd got rid of me when I went to Milan, but I didn't manage very well on my own. I'm not very well organised.'

'Are you sick?' Alice asked bluntly.

For a moment Tiffany looked startled, then she looked away. 'Not sick. Like I said, just not very well organised.' She stood up, keeping her hand on the arm of the sofa. 'Leo said you offered to take me shopping. He said I can go with you if he comes as well, but we mustn't tell Dr Grant. He doesn't like me leaving the house.'

Knowing she shouldn't interfere in family matters that didn't concern her, but unable to keep her mouth shut, Alice blurted out, 'He can't keep you a prisoner, you know, Tiffany.'

'I know he can't.' The girl shifted uncomfortably. 'But he's been good to me. He's away most of next week so if we go shopping then he won't know anything about it.' She looked up, her eyes pleading. 'Please, Alice. It's just easier if he doesn't know, then he won't worry about me.'

Telling herself again it was none of her business, Alice nodded. 'Okay, fine — next week it is. I'll sort the details out with your brother.'

She watched Tiffany leave the room. She was determined to get to the bottom of the mystery, one way or another. It was ridiculous, keeping a girl of Tiffany's age a virtual prisoner in the house. She should be out in the world, enjoying herself.

Alice worked on for another half hour until shouts and laughter drew her to the window. Someone had set up cricket stumps in the garden and Cassie was standing in front of the wicket with a plastic cricket bat in her hands. Peter Grant was the bowler, with Grace squatting behind the wicket, her hands ready to catch the ball. Dr Grant tossed the ball underhand and Cassie took a wild swipe, almost decapitating Grace, while the ball rolled away into the flowerbed. Dr Grant clapped his hands and roared with laughter.

Not wishing to miss all the fun, Alice stacked her work neatly and found her way out into the garden. Tiffany had joined them as a spectator and Leo appeared a few minutes later.

He looked at Alice and raised an eyebrow. 'I take it that work is over for the day, then?'

'Oh, don't be such a spoilsport, Leo,' Dr Grant said. He wiped his hands on his trousers and looked at his son curiously. 'Did we ever play cricket? We must have, I suppose. We seem to have all the equipment, but I don't remember playing.'

Grace straightened up with a little groan. 'I'm getting too old for games. You remember playing cricket, don't you, Leo?'

He nodded. 'Mostly with you, Gracie. Dad was away a lot.'

Alice wondered if that was what had broken up the marriage. An up-and-coming surgeon would have to spend a lot of time away from home, and a woman on her own would have to find ways to amuse herself.

'Lunch is inside today because it looked like rain,' Grace said. 'I'll just be a minute putting the dishes on the table.'

Tiffany took the older woman's arm. 'I'll come and help you.'

Dr Grant went to wash his hands, and Alice found herself left alone with Leo.

'Sorry,' she said. 'Did you want me to carry on working? I heard the noise and came out to see what was going on.'

He shook his head. 'I was just having fun with you. It's nearly lunchtime, anyway.'

Alice made sure that Dr Grant was nowhere in sight before she said quietly, 'Tiffany tells me you agreed to let her go shopping with me.'

'Yeah,' he said slowly. 'You don't mind if I come as well? Maybe Monday or Tuesday?'

'Tiffany said not to tell your father.'

'Better that way. Saves him worrying.'

'Why would he worry, though?' Alice persisted. 'She's a grown woman.'

'It's a long story.' Leo put a hand on her arm, giving her a sensation like an electric shock. 'Can you keep quiet about it for now, please? I'll explain when I can.'

She nodded as the doctor came back into the garden to tell them lunch was ready.

She could still feel the heat from Leo's hand on her arm and, right that moment, she would have agreed to practically anything. She told herself she was being really stupid, he wasn't interested in her, but that didn't help. For some reason Leo's touch had left her tingling all over. Wondering if her hair was standing on end or sending off sparks, she followed the doctor and his son back into the house.

★   ★   ★

Sitting next to Cassie, Alice got a complete rundown of the morning's

90

activities. Muffins had been baked, pastry rolled, and lemons liquidised. It had all been 'brilliant' and please could they stay here forever?

'Poor Mummy is at home, missing you.'

'She can come, too,' Cassie said airily. 'We can all live here in the castle. There's lots of room.'

Leo caught her eye from across the table and grinned. 'How about it? We could start a commune.'

Alice pursed her lips. 'Too risky. Think of the dragon.'

He should have asked what on earth she was talking about, but for some reason he didn't. 'One day I'll kill it,' he said wistfully, 'and save the princess.'

'You need a sword,' Cassie said gravely. 'The prince always has a sword to kill the dragon.'

Dr Grant had been listening to the conversation. 'I've got a book,' he said, 'with a picture of the sword Saint George used to kill his dragon.'

'Wow — can I see it?' Cassie asked him eagerly.

'It's on the top shelf in the library with my other rare books. When I have time, I'll see if I can find it. I've got quite a collection, including a first edition of *Alice's Adventures In Wonderland*.' He smiled at Cassie. 'The little girl in that book has the same name as your aunty.'

'Does the book have a dragon in it?'

'Something like a dragon. A Jabberwock. There's a picture of him as well, I think. When I get back from London next week we'll get the books down and have a look at them.'

'Please don't let Cassie touch them,' Alice said worriedly. 'She's only a little girl and she doesn't understand the value of an old book.'

'At the moment, all they're doing is gathering dust. Books are meant to be read. Besides, Leo tells me Cassie visits the library with you. She knows that books — all books — are valuable, don't you, Cassie?'

Cassie nodded solemnly. 'Specially books with dragons.'

Tiffany helped herself to a second helping of spaghetti. 'Did you read your children's books to Leo when he was little?' she asked the doctor.

'As Leo said, I was usually at the hospital when he went to bed — but his mother used to read them to him, I'm sure.'

Leo smiled, but didn't answer, and Alice began to feel just a little uncomfortable.

'Where do you live in LA?' she asked Tiffany, hoping to change the subject. 'Do you have your own place?'

'I did.' Tiffany glanced at her brother as if she was looking for help. 'But when I came back from Milan I stayed with Leo.' Her smile was a little tight. 'It's cheaper for both of us.'

Leo reached over to pour Alice more Sangria, but she put her hand over her glass. 'Sorry — I have to drive home with Cassie, so one glass is plenty.'

'Oh, you needn't worry — there's very little alcohol in this,' the doctor assured her. 'One of us often has to drive somewhere after lunch.'

'Except for me,' Tiffany said, with a touch of bitterness.

Dr Grant stood up and pushed his chair back under the table. 'You know very well you can't drive in this country, Tiffany. You don't have a licence.'

'But I could . . . '

'No, you couldn't, so let's hear no more of it.' He screwed up his paper napkin and dropped it on to his plate. 'In just over a week, you can do what you damn well please.'

Leo watched his father leave the room, and laughed. 'Good old Dad, he's just the same. It doesn't take much to upset him.'

'I'm sorry, Leo.' Tiffany looked near to tears. 'That was all my fault.'

Leo patted her hand. 'Forget it. It wasn't your fault at all. Just my father being his usual self.' He noticed that Alice was on her feet and he immediately got up himself to help Cassie down from her chair.

'Sorry about all that,' he said disarmingly as he walked with them to the door.

'Oh, don't be silly, Leo. That's what families are all about. It's the first time your father has met his stepdaughter, isn't it? There's bound to be some friction between them.'

Leo sighed. 'I wish that's all it was.'

* * *

Cassie was quiet in the car going home and Alice asked if she was all right.

'I think he's already got a princess,' Cassie said glumly. 'Tiffany's really pretty, and she has long hair just like a storybook princess.'

'She's Leo's sister, and she lives with him already. He won't have to slay a dragon to rescue her, will he? I think you're still in with a chance.'

Cassie bounced on her booster seat. 'So I can still live in his castle one day? Tiffany won't mind. She really likes me.'

Alice reached backwards to pat her niece's knee. 'Everyone likes you, darling.' She put her hand back on the wheel to make a right turn. 'Just don't touch the doctor's books.'

* * *

Leo found his father in the living room watching cricket on the television. Dr Grant didn't look up, and Leo sighed. His father had always been the same; moody and bad-tempered one minute, and perfectly fine the next. As a boy, Leo had never known what mood to expect, and it didn't surprise him when his mother eventually got fed up with it all and walked out.

She had already met a man who told her how wonderful she was and bought her expensive gifts. He was single and wealthy and asked her to live in America with him — but he had expected her to leave her son behind. When she turned up with an eleven-year-old in tow and told him she was pregnant, he got cold feet.

He agreed to buy her an apartment in Los Angeles if she'd let him off the hook, and she agreed. When Tiffany was born, she sold the apartment and bought a fairly modest house in a nice part of town.

In spite of everything, Leo had managed to settle in at his new school and when his baby sister arrived he found, much to his surprise, that he adored her. Right from the start, he had taken her under his wing.

The trouble was that she was still there.

He watched the television in silence for a few minutes, wondering how to bring up the subject that was bothering him.

He didn't know his father. He probably never had. All his memories were of a rather distant man, with little time for a child, and he was surprised by the way his father treated Cassie, especially as he seemed to genuinely like the little girl.

When it became obvious his father had no intention of starting a conversation, Leo moved in front of the television screen. 'I need to speak to you, Dad.'

His father reached for the remote and turned the sound down. 'Speak away.'

'Go easy on Tiffany. She's scared and lonely. She needs your support in this.'

Dr Grant stared past him at the screen. A batsman had just been run out.

'I was under the impression I was giving her all the support I possibly could, even to the point of putting her at the top of my operating list. If she needs more she'll have to get it from her mother. Caroline has informed me she is arriving next week.'

'Mother? She's coming here? Why would she do that? I told her I could handle things.'

'Because she doesn't trust you, I would imagine. You're too tied up with your writing to be objective. You'd let the girl wander off and get lost if you had your way, and timing is vital, you know that; besides which, she's not safe out on her own. You should know that as well.'

'You think I don't?' Leo said wearily. 'I know better than anyone how difficult it is to keep Tiffany safe, but she just needs a little slack on that rope you've put round her neck. She's eighteen, and she's had to cope with her diabetes for years . . . '

Dr Grant held up a hand. 'She obviously doesn't cope, though, does she? That's why she's in this mess.'

Leo could feel his frustration turning to anger. It was time he left. 'When is Mother arriving?'

Dr Grant shrugged. 'I have no idea.' He turned the television sound back up with a wry smile. 'Grace won't be pleased.'

Leo went to find Tiffany. He wasn't sure of what his sister's reaction would be to Caroline's imminent arrival. There had been a great deal of friction between the two women before Tiffany had left for England.

'Why?' Tiffany asked, white-faced. 'Why is she coming? She said she was too busy. I don't want her here. You know she's going to cause trouble. She'll argue with your father all the time.' She looked near to tears. 'I want to go shopping with Alice like we planned.'

Leo wondered how Alice would cope with his mother. If he counted Grace, there would be four strong-willed women in the house at the same time, and that didn't bode well for anyone. His father could take off for the hospital, but Leo knew he was going to be left behind to attempt to keep the peace.

'Look, it's Sunday tomorrow. I'll take you out for a drive. And we'll still do the shopping trip on Monday.' He smiled at his sister. 'If we leave before our mother arrives, she can't very well stop us, can she?'

Tiffany gave him a watery smile in return. 'She'll probably lock me in my room when she gets here.'

'Never mind.' He brushed a tear from Tiffany's cheek. 'By then you'll only have a few more days to go.'

6

As Alice parked outside the house on the Monday morning, Dr Grant was loading a suitcase into his black Mercedes.

'Good morning, Alice,' he said distractedly. 'Tell Leo I'll try and get back before Caroline arrives.'

Before Alice could ask any questions, he slammed the car door and drove away down the drive.

Caroline? Who was Caroline? The doctor had left the front door open, so she let herself in and went in search of Leo and Tiffany. She found them both in the library.

'Has he gone?' Tiffany asked eagerly. 'I'm ready to go right now! We don't want to waste any time.'

Leo looked as if he might be having second thoughts. 'For goodness' sake, Tiffany — give Dad a chance to get out of the village. What if he comes back for something?'

'He won't. He's catching the ten-fifteen train. He told me.'

Leo looked at his watch and rolled his eyes at Alice. 'Did you bring Cassie?' he asked.

She shook her head. 'No, Lauren can manage her today. Besides, you wouldn't have wanted her with you.'

'Why not?' Tiffany asked. 'She seems very well-behaved.'

'Oh, she is. But I've vowed never to take her clothes shopping again, unless the clothes are for her. She has an opinion on everything, most of it bad, and she includes everyone who happens to be in the shop. She once told a woman who was trying on a dress that she should get a bigger size. That went down like the Titanic, I can tell you.' Even the memory of that encounter made Alice shudder. 'No, believe me — we're better off without her.'

'Ah well.' Tiffany waved a gold credit card. 'Full right up to the top! I haven't had a chance to spend any of it since I arrived here, so I'll buy you something pretty as well, Alice.'

It would be silly to take offence, Alice decided; Tiffany meant her offer in the nicest possible way. But she did wonder, as she climbed into the back of Leo's rented car, if she looked in need of a new wardrobe.

She was wearing skinny black jeans and a loose purple top, a black cardigan tied round her neck. She had thought she looked sort of designer casual — until she saw Tiffany.

The younger girl's cream silk trousers and bright orange shirt looked amazing, but you would need to be almost six feet tall to show them off. The oversize sunglasses added a further touch of class.

Alice consoled herself with the thought that at her height, she had more of a choice in men. In fact, anyone over five feet four was taller than she was.

'Who's Caroline?' she asked, remembering Dr Grant's parting words.

Tiffany looked back over her shoulder at Alice. 'Our mother. She's flying to England for some reason.'

'You mean here, to this house?' Alice asked, a touch of panic in her voice. She still had editing to do.

'Yes, here to this house,' Tiffany said bitterly. 'And I have absolutely no idea why.'

Leo was looking for road signs. 'I would imagine it's because she's worried about you.'

'Why is she worried about me all of a sudden? She wasn't worried about me before we left for England.'

'Please don't keep asking questions, Tiffany, it's distracting me. I'm trying to drive a stick-shift on the wrong side of the road.' Leo saw the sign for the shopping centre and pulled into the left-hand lane. 'I have no idea why she's flying all the way over here. I can only assume that she wants to see you before you go into hospital. I suggest we leave this conversation until we get home again.'

Tiffany didn't answer, and Alice thought it would be unwise to question further. So Tiffany was due to go into hospital! Her suspicions about her fragile health could be right. But it seemed odd that their mother should suddenly decide to make such a long journey when she had evidently known beforehand. Another mystery to add to what was getting to be quite a long list.

Alice had to bite her lip while Leo parked the car. He was used to automatic transmission, and changing gear was obviously proving to be a bit of a problem, although he would never admit it. Luckily the hire-car had a warning system that beeped if he got too close to anything, otherwise there might well have been a nasty accident. A couple of times she almost offered to park it for him, but then she decided that her offer, however well-meant, might not go down very well.

Once inside the shopping precinct, Leo tucked Tiffany's arm in his. 'Don't let go,' he warned, 'or I shall take you straight back to the car.'

He treats her like a child, Alice thought, feeling sorry for the girl. Tiffany was eighteen, not two years old.

Tiffany was delighted with the small designer shops. 'I thought you could only buy these names in London,' she exclaimed, picking up a leather hand-bag and peering at the label. 'Is this real, or is it a knock-off? I can't read the price.'

Alice looked over the girl's shoulder and gasped. 'Would you really spend all that money on one handbag?'

Tiffany sighed. 'Don't tell me the price, or I'll have to remind myself I'm not working at the moment.'

Alice was ready to give up after two hours, and could see Leo was feeling the strain when he suggested lunch.

'Good idea,' Tiffany agreed, letting go of his arm. 'But I need the rest-room first.'

'Me too,' Alice said.

Leo looked worried. 'Mind you come straight back.'

'Oh, for goodness' sake, Leo,' Tiffany retorted impatiently. 'I can manage. Alice will see that I don't get lost in there.'

'He does fuss rather a lot, doesn't he?' Alice said, as they walked away from Leo. 'Is there a reason he worries about you all the time?'

Tiffany stopped walking. 'Like what? What did Leo tell you?'

'Nothing,' Alice said hastily, wishing she'd kept her mouth shut. 'He didn't say anything at all. I just wondered, because you're a model, if you'd once had anorexia or something. I noticed Leo's always watching how much you eat.'

Tiffany looked blank for a minute, then she smiled. 'No, I don't have anorexia, Alice. I'm diabetic, and not always very good at managing it. I really screwed up when I was in Milan. In fact, I nearly died because I forgot my insulin and didn't eat enough. I got sent home by my agency and I have to sort myself out or they'll drop me. Leo worries about me and he's trying to help, bless him. That's all.'

That explained a lot, Alice thought. No wonder Leo was overprotective. 'I'm sorry, Tiffany. I didn't mean to pry.'

The girl shrugged. 'No problem.'

Alice pushed open the door to the ladies'. 'It must have been pretty scary being in a foreign country on your own. Were the other models nice to you?'

'I suppose, but I don't make friends easily. I've got lots of friends in England, though.' She grinned. 'On Facebook. At least here you speak the same language.' Another grin. 'Well — almost. Not quite.'

'Of course. Facebook is great, isn't it? You can have friends all over the world.'

★　★　★

When they returned, Leo wasn't in the place they'd left him, and Alice felt Tiffany's hand tighten on her arm.

'Where is he? He promised he'd wait here.'

'He won't be far away,' Alice said soothingly. Tiffany's grip had practically cut off the circulation to her lower arm. 'He knows where to find us, doesn't he?'

Leo reappeared a few minutes later. 'Sorry. I was looking at something in a mountaineering shop window, over there.'

'You said you'd wait *here*.' There was a little hitch of panic in Tiffany's voice.

'I said I'm sorry.' He took his sister's hand and gave it a rub. 'Let's go and eat.'

They found a restaurant that served Italian food and Tiffany was soon smiling again.

'I need to get those shoes I saw.' She was halfway through a plate of tortellini with crab and lobster. 'And maybe that grey cashmere sweater for Mom.' She smiled at her brother. 'We need to put her in a good mood, and cashmere will probably do it. Besides, she's not used to the English weather. She'll expect it to be hot this time of year and she won't bring anything warm to wear.'

'It *is* hot for this time of year,' Alice said, and then laughed. 'But probably not as hot as LA.'

'It's going to be really uncomfortable with her in the same house as Dad.' Leo pushed his plate away. 'I can't believe she's doing this.' He looked at Tiffany. 'I hope you took your medication today.'

'It's not 'medication',' Tiffany said, making speech marks with her fingers. 'It's insulin. And yes, I did inject in the restroom, and you don't have to be diplomatic, because I told Alice I have diabetes.' She put her spoon and fork on her plate. 'And I ate every scrap of that lovely pasta, so you don't have to nag me about that, either.'

'Shoes, then,' Leo said with a smile. 'And a cashmere sweater for our mother.'

* * *

The day had gone well, Alice thought with a happy little sigh. Tiffany had insisted on buying her a pair of pretty earrings with a dangly bracelet to match, and she had treated herself to a small clutch bag in pink leather. She was full of good food, and the sun was still shining. Tiffany was in the back of the car dozing, which left Alice sitting in the front next to Leo.

She glanced sideways at him, noticing how the sunlight caught the gold in his hair.

It would be so easy to imagine she was alone with him in the car, and that they were going somewhere romantic. A small country inn, maybe, with a four-poster bed and satin sheets . . .

No! That was going way too far. Anyway, satin sheets would be slippery — and they would probably both fall out of bed. The thought was so silly, it made her smile.

She had her head against the back of the seat with her eyes closed, and for a moment she didn't realise they had stopped. She opened her eyes to find Leo half turned round in his seat looking intently at her.

'What?' she said uneasily. His eyes were such an incredible blue, they shouldn't be allowed. She sat up and unfastened her seat belt. 'Why are you looking at me like that?'

'Because you look quite beautiful when you're asleep, and I was thinking that perhaps I should kiss you. Isn't that what a prince is supposed to do? Kiss the sleeping beauty?'

'Tiffany . . . ' she said faintly, reaching for the door handle.

'My sister is fast asleep in the back.'

'I might turn into a frog.' She gave a nervous little laugh. 'If I were you, I wouldn't risk it.'

But he was already leaning towards her, so she decided to give in gracefully. She closed her eyes in anticipation but opened them again when she heard him curse.

'Damn! I'd forgotten this was a stick-shift.'

Blocked in by the gear lever, he cursed again, and Alice heard Tiffany stir on the back seat. 'Are we home?'

Alice giggled. 'I think the prince has been well and truly defeated by a gear lever. Perhaps you should have brought your sword with you.'

'Don't get too complacent,' he told her. 'This is just a postponement, not a defeat.'

Tiffany gathered her bags together and climbed sleepily out of the car. 'Thank you, Alice,' she called over her shoulder as she headed towards the house. 'That was such fun. I hope you're not too tired.'

'Not at all,' Alice answered brightly. She was twenty-five, not eighty-five, for goodness' sake! 'When exactly is your mother arriving?' she asked Leo. 'Do you still want me to come over here tomorrow?'

He looked astonished. 'Of course! I need you now more than ever. I can't possibly manage my sister and my mother by myself. And Grace will be on the warpath. She's never forgiven Mum for whisking me away to America.'

He got out of the car and held the door for Alice.

'I expect Grace missed you. You said she looked after you a lot when you were little.'

She'd miss him as well, when he went back to America, she admitted to herself.

Tiffany had disappeared into the house and Alice knew she ought to be getting into her car and heading for home, but somehow she seemed rooted to the spot.

'I need to get home. Lauren probably needs me.'

He took a step towards her and she still didn't move.

'Not half as much as I do.'

Another step brought him within touching distance. It felt as if her senses were on fire.

'If I remember rightly, we have a little unfinished business to attend to before you leave.'

The sound of a car on gravel had her moving away. 'I can hear a car coming up the drive. It's probably your father.'

'You could be right.' He sighed. 'Foiled again. We'll put this on hold for the moment, but I won't forget. I hope Tiff's had time to get rid of the shopping evidence.'

'Why would your father mind her shopping?' Alice asked. 'If she can handle Milan on her own, she's not likely to get lost in Breakwater shopping centre — and she seems to have her diabetes under control.'

Leo managed to avoid answering as his father drove up and parked in front of the house. Dr Grant got out and then walked round to open the passenger door.

The woman who climbed out was an older version of Tiffany. Tall and enviously skinny, with a fall of red-gold hair, designer suit and six-inch heels, she made Alice want to run and hide.

Leo walked towards the woman with a rather forced smile.

'Hello, Mother.'

The woman closed the car door.

'Leo, darling.' Alice noticed there was no attempt at a kiss or a hug. 'Where's Tiffany? I need to talk to her. I think she's being unnecessarily hasty and we should all sit down together and discuss everything. I keep telling her there are other alternatives.'

She seemed to suddenly notice Alice. 'And this is . . . ?'

'I'm the editor. Leo's editor. Of his book. Temporarily, that is.' Alice took a breath. *Shut up while you're still ahead* had always been good advice. 'I was just going.'

Leo smiled sympathetically. 'I'll see you tomorrow morning, then, Alice. Same time.'

Alice thought he was going to say something else, but when he didn't she walked over to her car and opened the door.

She ought to say goodbye, but she had no idea whether Caroline still used the name Grant, so she gave a silly, rather hesitant little wave to them all, and quickly drove away feeling slightly stupid.

She arrived home just in time to avoid a disaster. Lauren was dealing with her last client of the day, trying to wash the woman's hair while keeping an anxious eye on Cassie.

'Thank goodness you're back, Alice. Can you take Cassie out of here, please? She keeps picking up my bottles and I have no idea what she's got now.'

Alice plucked the small bottle out of Cassie's hand. 'Deep Bronze permanent. I'm glad she didn't take the top off.'

'I never take the tops off,' Cassie replied indignantly. 'Mummy told me not to. I'm just styling Molly's hair.'

Alice noticed that the unfortunate doll's hair was now only about an inch long all over, but it wasn't a bad cut, considering.

She stood the bottle back on the shelf while Lauren apologised to her client. 'I'm so sorry, Barbara. I won't keep you much longer.'

The woman didn't seem all that concerned, but she had her head tilted back and couldn't see what was going on.

Alice found a dustpan and brush and swept up the doll's hair.

'Come on, Cassie. Let's go and get dinner started.'

'Can we have fish and chips?' her niece asked hopefully.

Alice looked at Lauren. 'Shall I take her to the chip shop?'

'Do you mind?'

'Not at all.' Alice took Cassie's hand. 'Put your jacket on, though, Cass, it's getting chilly now that the sun's gone in.'

*   *   *

By the time they got back Lauren had almost finished with her client, so Alice put the fish and chips in the oven to keep warm and Cassie helped her set the table.

Lauren came in ten minutes later

looking exhausted.

'Cassie's been really good, and I know she's fairly sensible, but most of the stuff in those bottles is lethal and I worry all the time she's in the salon.'

'I know. I'm sorry I'm so late back. I've got lots to tell you, but we'd better wait until there's one less pair of ears. Cassie repeats everything she hears.'

Lauren laughed. 'She's just being a typical woman.'

Cassie dunked a chip in tomato ketchup. 'I can keep secrets. Aunty Alice told me what she got you for your birthday, remember? That was a secret.'

'But you *told* me,' Lauren protested. 'You're not supposed to tell secrets.'

'But you were happy when I told you. You said it was just what you wanted. You were happy for a whole week.'

Lauren smiled at her daughter. 'You're quite right. I had a whole week of happiness because you told me, instead of just one day. It was very kind of you.'

Alice had never managed to understand the way her sister's mind worked, and now it seemed Cassie had inherited her mother's strange sense of logic.

'I take it neither of you like surprises, then?' she said.

'I hate them.' Lauren started clearing the table. 'You miss all that lovely looking-forward-to time.'

'Like I said before, you're both weird.'

⋆ ⋆ ⋆

Once Cassie was safely tucked up in bed, Lauren poured a glass of wine for each of them and sat beside her sister on the sofa. 'So! How did the shopping spree go?'

Alice took a sip of her wine. This was the time she liked best, when she could sit and relax and talk to her sister about her day. 'It was great. I found out why Leo fusses about Tiffany so much. She's a type-one diabetic. She got sent home from Milan because she wasn't handling it very well, and the agency will sack her if she doesn't get her act together. I think this is her last chance.'

'Poor kid.' Lauren sighed. 'I can imagine how I would feel if Cassie had to cope with something like that. It can't have been easy for her, particularly in the modelling profession. With diabetes you can't cut out meals.'

'Evidently her mother wasn't much help, either, according to Leo. She seems to think the odd piece of chocolate cake can't do any harm, almost as if Tiffany's making a fuss about nothing. Leo had to look after his sister when she was small and I think it was a relief when she took up modelling and went to Milan, but she obviously didn't manage very well on her own.'

'She was quite young to be working in a foreign country. What sort of person is her mother, I wonder?'

'I'll find out tomorrow. She turned up just as I was leaving.'

'Wow! Was she expected, then? Did anyone know she was even coming?'

'She phoned Dr Grant yesterday. It was quite a shock for Leo, though — and Tiffany didn't seem too pleased, either. The mother's tall, with hair more gold than red, and she looked fantastic, even though she'd just got off a plane.'

'She'd make sure of that. She was meeting her ex for the first time in twenty-odd years. She had to look her best.'

'The doctor didn't seem that put out. He must have gone to the airport to meet her. I just hope there isn't too much friction at the house tomorrow.' Alice refilled both their glasses. 'I think I almost got kissed by the prince.'

Lauren was silent for a moment. 'The words 'think' and 'almost' worry me a little — but you didn't turn into a frog.'

'I did tell him I might.'

'Was that what put him off?'

Alice laughed and shook her head. 'No. First of all he was baulked by the gear lever and then his father turned up. It really wasn't his day.'

'There's always tomorrow, I suppose.

Will it affect you working for him? He's not going to be chasing you round the desk all the time, is he?'

'I wish; but unfortunately he's not like that. Business is business as far as he's concerned, he's always been entirely professional, and yes, if I let him kiss me it probably would affect our working relationship, so I intend to keep him at arm's length until I finish my job, and then we'll see.'

Alice took a sip of wine and continued, 'Actually, the book is quite good. It's action-packed and a tad ridiculous at times, but good fun to read, and I like his heroine. If she decides to go after something, she won't back off.'

'Do we get discount copies?' Lauren asked, and then yawned. 'Today has been a bit fraught, to say the least, so I think I'll get to bed.'

'Once I've made quite sure we've got enough milk, I'll make myself a mug of cocoa.' Alice picked up the empty glasses. 'Sleep tight.'

Lauren paused in the doorway. 'The boiler man came round again today, just to check everything was okay. I told him we might be able to afford a new boiler soon.'

'Hopefully, yes, but why did he call here again? I hope he didn't charge you for a call-out.'

'Oh, no.' For some reason Lauren's face had gone pink. 'He was just making sure we had hot water and everything. There was no charge.'

Alice frowned. 'Well, just make sure we don't get a bill.'

'He was just being kind. And he said he was passing our house anyway, so he thought he'd make sure the boiler was still working. He knows I need hot water for my business.'

'And how would he know that? You must have had a long chat with him when he came to check the boiler.'

'If you must know, I made him a cup of tea. I didn't think there was any harm in that.'

'Aha! That's probably why he called

again today. It had nothing to do with our boiler. He wanted another free cup of tea.'

'Why do you always assume people have an ulterior motive? Some people are just plain nice.'

Lauren left the room without saying goodnight, which was unusual for her.

Alice looked at the closed door, a surprised expression on her face. *What had brought that on?* she wondered.

Lauren and the boiler man? Surely not. She tried to remember if she had ever actually seen the repair man. She could remember an old man who used to call when their mother was alive, but this must be someone new. When she had a minute she'd check the boiler repair company on her computer. You could never be too careful.

While she was heating the milk for her cocoa, Alice thought about the coming day. She wasn't exactly looking forward to it, but it should certainly be interesting.

7

The weather had changed by the morning and a thin drizzle slicked the roads. The rain matched Alice's mood. Overnight she had come to the conclusion that she was just a pleasant diversion for Leo. He was probably as bored as his sister and looking forward to getting back to LA.

She got out of the car and prepared to make a run for the front door. Perhaps the ex-Mrs Grant wouldn't stay long if this weather kept up.

To her surprise, Leo opened the front door himself. 'I'm doing Grace's job today.'

'Where's Grace? Not ill, I hope.'

'Not unless sulking counts as an illness. I think she's on strike. She put breakfast on the table this morning without saying a word and I haven't seen her since. You should have brought

Cassie with you. I'm sure she'd handle my mother better than any of us.'

'You're probably right.' Alice let him take her wet jacket and hang it on an old-fashioned coat rack. 'I didn't want to make matters worse, so Lauren changed her appointments for today, but I may have to bring Cassie with me tomorrow.'

'That was our arrangement, and she'll keep Grace happy. That's where the main problem lies. Grace won't speak to my mother, which makes things difficult to say the least. I fully intend to lock us both in the library and not open the door until lunch time.'

He saw Alice's alarmed expression, and laughed. 'I have no intention of seducing you; not in the library, anyway.'

She gave an exaggerated sigh of relief. 'I'm so glad. I was afraid I might have to hand in my notice.'

'My mother has scheduled a family meeting for this afternoon, which means we have a lot of work to get through this morning. You're safe for the time being.'

'Well, in that case, I'll go home for lunch today, then, if you don't mind,' she told him. 'Lauren really needs me.'

He opened the library door for her. 'Coward.'

★   ★   ★

Alice left just before lunch and Leo heaved a sigh of relief. He had managed to keep her away from his mother for the time being, but he knew that wouldn't last.

When he entered the conservatory, Caroline was already there, a glass in her hand.

'Water,' she said, when she saw Leo. 'I won't drink alcohol in front of Tiffany.'

'She's a diabetic, mother,' Leo muttered, 'not an alcoholic.'

'But she shouldn't drink. You told me that.'

'She can have an occasional glass of

wine . . . ' He saw his mother was about to argue and held up his hand. 'But you're probably right. It's best not to drink in front of her.'

Anything to keep the peace, he thought wearily.

It was starting all over again. Put the two women together and there would always be trouble. Add Grace and his father to the equation, and any trouble was likely to escalate into something far worse.

It had taken him months to talk Tiffany into coming to England, now his mother was about to undo all his hard work with a few well-chosen words. Family meeting, be damned! He was about to witness the start of World War Three.

'Where's your little editor? I thought she worked all day.'

'She's here for four hours, normally, but I let her off early today because of your meeting.' He poured himself a glass of white wine from the bottle on the table, ignoring the look he got.

'Why did you really come over to England, Mother? The last thing we want to do is spook Tiff at this late stage.'

'I'm worried about her. I checked on the Internet and I think we should look at alternatives, that's all. An operation is simply too radical.'

Leo shushed his mother as Tiffany came into the room.

'Hi, Mom.' Tiffany walked over to the table and looked at the food. 'If I eat any more salad I'll turn into a rabbit. Can't Grace think of something more filling? I shall be hungry again in half an hour.'

'I agree, dear. Grace never was very innovative where food is concerned.'

'There's chicken and sliced beef as well as salad,' Leo pointed out. 'If you want something special, just tell Grace. I'm sure she'll do her best to get it for you.'

'Never mind.' Caroline picked up a warm bread roll and started to butter it. 'We'll eat out tonight. There must be somewhere that serves decent food.'

Dr Grant walked into the room and nodded to them before taking his place at the head of the table. He topped up Caroline's water glass and filled his own.

'I suggest we eat before we start any sort of discussion,' he said. 'I brought the relevant papers with me so you can see exactly what I have planned, Caroline.'

Caroline filled her plate with food. 'Why didn't you have this procedure done in America, Tiffany? The hospitals are far more up-to-date . . . ' She looked disparagingly at her ex-husband. 'And so are the doctors.'

'I won't discuss this while we're eating, Caroline,' the doctor told her sharply. 'Tell me about your shopping trip, Tiffany. Grace tells me you went to the Brakewater centre with Alice.'

'Leo came as well, he wouldn't let me go without him.' Tiffany looked at her mother. 'You should go, too, while you're here. It's better than the mall we go to back home. There are more designer names. French, English, Italian. We had a real good time.'

Between them, Leo and his father succeeded in keeping the small talk going until lunch was finished. Grace managed to serve the coffee without speaking at all, and then started clearing the table.

'Shall we stay in here?' the doctor asked. 'It's brighter than the lounge.' He looked at Caroline. 'Do you want Tiffany to hear what you have to tell us?'

'I'm staying, anyway.' Tiffany pushed her coffee cup away. 'You can't discuss my future without me. Besides, I don't know what this dreadful fuss is all about. I've already decided what I'm going to do, and Dr Grant has everything already arranged.'

'I just think an operation is a bit drastic, that's all,' Caroline said. 'Something that needs to be discussed fully. Do you realise if anything goes wrong, you could go blind?'

'She's already going blind,' the doctor said quietly. 'She has a degenerative eye disease.'

'Poof! You can't know that for sure, and there are alternatives. I've done my homework, and I've heard laser surgery can be done in a few minutes as an outpatient procedure. Why does she need to go into hospital for an operation? Why all the fuss? All you're doing is frightening Tiffany when she needs your reassurance.'

Caroline turned to face her daughter. 'You should have this done back home.'

'I can't, Mom. I'm on the front cover of Elle as face of the year, and you can be sure someone will recognise me. But no one over here knows me — not yet, anyway — and Dr Grant can keep me out of sight at his hospital. I daren't let the agency find out I'm having trouble with my sight. They'll decide I'm too much trouble and get rid of me. I'm supposed to be taking this vacation to get my diabetes sorted. Do you know how long it's taken me to get this far?'

She looked near to tears. 'You should be pleased, Mom, Dr Grant is doing all this for free.'

'I'm taking her to the hospital with me tomorrow for a final check-up. By the end of the week, this will all be over and you can go back home.'

Leo suddenly realised that he didn't want to go home. Not yet. He had unfinished business to attend to. A princess who needed a kiss to wake her up.

'If my mother can take Tiffany back with her, I may stay over for a bit longer. There's still some editing to do on the book.'

'No! You have to come back with us, Leo.' Tiffany was on her feet. 'I don't want you to stay here. I need you with me.'

'I'll be here for your operation,' he said soothingly, wishing that, just for once, his sister could manage her life without him. 'I'll be at the hospital when you wake up, and then you'll be able to see just fine and you won't need me around any more.'

'No, Leo!' Her voice had risen to a wail. 'You have to promise you'll come back with me or I won't have it done.'

Leo looked at his father for support, but all he got was a raised eyebrow.

He couldn't blame the man. Dr Grant had put himself out for a stepdaughter he had never met, booked her into the private section of the hospital where he worked, and thoroughly disrupted his orderly life.

Grace was refusing to speak to anyone, and his mother was being particularly awkward. No wonder the doctor wanted to get rid of them all again as quickly as possible.

'Wait until you're out of hospital and then I'll try and get the book finished in time to come back with you.'

Tiffany shook her head like a spoiled child. Any moment now she would start stamping her feet, he thought.

'You have to promise me, Leo. You must promise me right now that you'll fly back with me.'

What was he supposed to do? He wished he'd asked Alice to stay — she would have sorted out this mess with a few well-chosen words — but he couldn't allow Tiffany to blackmail him.

'I'm not making a promise I might have to break,' he told her. 'I work as well, and I have a deadline for this book. Perhaps if we let Mother look at the schedule for the operation, she won't be so worried. It's a procedure my father has done lots of times. The operation carries very little risk, but if you don't have it done you will eventually go blind.'

'I can't see very much now,' Tiffany said petulantly. 'Going blind won't make that much difference.'

'Believe me, it will.' The doctor's voice was suddenly filled with a quiet anger. 'You should meet some of the people on the NHS waiting list.'

Tiffany got to her feet and walked out of the room, her lunch uneaten. Leo wished wholeheartedly that he could just switch off and let someone else do the worrying for once.

He wondered sometimes whether he had sent Tiffany off to Milan for his own benefit; purely out of selfishness. Perhaps if he had stopped her going, this would never have happened. He had been so relieved at the thought of getting on with his writing without having to worry about her, he had even helped her pack her bags and driven her to the airport. He told himself fiercely that he was entitled to a life — but that didn't help. Not now, when his baby sister might go blind.

He hoped he wouldn't have to choose between keeping Tiffany happy or staying with Alice, because he knew what his choice would have to be.

* * *

Alice drove along in the sunshine with Cassie beside her while her stomach bubbled audibly with fear. This was silly. She had tackled women much more formidable than Caroline.

She thought of the mothers she'd faced at school. Woman incensed with fury because little Tommy hadn't got a gold star and Bobby from down the road had. Women who looked prepared to commit murder when Alice had the temerity to mention homework that hadn't been handed in.

All of them were mothers — just like Caroline.

'You will be good, won't you, Cassie?'

'You already said that.' Cassie wriggled on her booster seat. 'I'm always good.'

Wishing she could believe that, Alice parked outside the house. This time Grace greeted them at the front door and Cassie hugged the woman round her ample middle. Grace picked the little girl up and sat her on her hip.

'We'll make more cakes,' she said, heading off down the hall. 'We stay away from that woman and make cakes.'

'What woman?' Cassie asked, looking back at Alice as Grace whisked her away to the kitchen.

Alice didn't hear Grace's reply. She turned round when she heard a movement behind her, only to be confronted by Caroline.

'So you're Leo's editor. You look too young for such a highly responsible job.'

'I'm a school teacher,' Alice said, feeling wrong-footed already. 'I'm just helping Leo out while he's here in England.'

'Ah. I see. And is he paying you for this help of yours?'

'Yes, he is.' Alice somehow felt the need to recover her dignity in front of this woman. 'I certainly don't work for free.'

'Good for you. I thought that you might be doing more than just editing his book. I saw the way he was looking at you when I arrived yesterday.'

Alice felt her face growing hot. This woman was nothing like the mothers at school; she was far worse.

'If that were true,' she retorted, 'he's not paying me nearly enough. Now, if you'll excuse me, I have to get to work.'

When Alice opened the library door, Leo looked up from his desk, saw the look on her face, and closed his eyes wearily.

'You met my mother.'

Alice was beginning to find the situation more funny than annoying. 'In the fairy story, there are always three characters, aren't there? The prince, the princess, and the . . . '

'Dragon?' Leo finished for her.

'I'm sorry,' she said with a giggle. 'I was thinking more of the wicked stepmother, but I shouldn't be rude about your mother. She mistook me for your English distraction. She thought the term 'editor' was a euphemism for something more interesting.'

'My mother is obviously more observant than I thought.'

Alice refused to rise to the bait.

'I think I explained our relationship to her satisfaction. I brought Cassie with me today, but Grace carried her off to the kitchen, which is probably just as well.'

She looked at his desk. 'It seems we have a lot of work to get through today.'

★ ★ ★

Alice was surprised when Leo announced that it was lunchtime. The morning had gone well. She was beginning to understand the way in which Leo used words, and editing his work had become easier. Sometimes she found herself so caught up in the story, she had to backtrack to make sure she hadn't missed any errors. There was more depth to his writing than she had at first thought. One of his books might make an interesting project for discussion, she decided — at least with her older students. They might actually enjoy reading it.

She left Leo to tidy up while she collected Cassie from the kitchen. 'No playing in the garden today, then?'

'Mrs Grant, she sits on the terrace and reads a book all morning.' Grace shrugged. 'The little one is quite happy making jam tarts.'

'Did you make those all by yourself?' Alice watched Cassie put the last round of pastry into a bun tin and drop in a spoonful of jam. 'They're brilliant!'

Cassie licked the jam spoon and smiled smugly. 'You can't make jam tarts, can you?'

Alice shook her head. 'No, I can't. You'll have to teach me.'

'First of all, I have to teach Mister Leo. That's what Grace calls him, but he's still a prince, isn't he?'

'Of course he is, and you're still a princess, but even princesses have to eat, so let's go and find lunch.'

Grace picked up the bun tin and popped it in the oven. 'Don't forget to take your tarts home.'

'I made six,' Cassie said, hopping along beside Alice. 'That's two each.'

'Wow. You've learnt a lot since you started school. How many will be left if I eat one?'

Triumphantly, Cassie held up her sticky hand, fingers spread wide. 'Five!'

Leo caught up with them. 'Hello,

Cassie. You having a good day, baby girl?'

Cassie gave him a scornful look. 'I'm not a baby. I just made six jam tarts.'

'Absolute proof of maturity. I apologise, Cassie.'

He caught Alice's arm to delay her progress. 'I just came to warn you, mother and Tiff are at it again, so lunch could be difficult, and I really need to explain what's going on. I should have told you this morning but we were getting on so well with the editing, I forgot.'

He was about to say more but Cassie had pushed open the door to the conservatory and several pairs of eyes were now looking at them.

Alice walked into the room with as much bravado as she could muster. She slid into a chair while Leo lifted Cassie on to her seat and sat down himself. The air would need to be cut with a very sharp knife, and she wondered if anyone was going to speak or whether the meal was going to proceed in silence.

'You've met Alice, haven't you, Caroline?' the doctor asked.

'Briefly.' Caroline shot him a look. 'I think we should keep family matters to ourselves for now, don't you, particularly while we're eating. Is your editing work nearly finished?' she asked Alice coolly.

Alice nodded, pleased to have a question she could actually answer. 'Yes, almost. Another couple of days should do it.'

'Tiffany wants to take me to the shopping mall. I don't drive, but I guess we can get a cab.'

Alice glanced nervously at Leo. 'I could drop you off, if you like, then you'd only have to get a taxi back. When were you planning on going?'

Tiffany looked up, taking part in the conversation for the first time. 'Tomorrow?'

'You know you can't go tomorrow, Tiffany,' the doctor told her. 'You're coming with me.'

'Am I?' She was wearing her outsize

145

sunglasses and her eyes were hidden. 'What if I've changed my mind?'

Alice saw a muscle twitch in Dr Grant's jaw. 'Cassie made some jam tarts today,' she volunteered. 'Didn't you, Cassie?'

Cassie had been sitting quietly trying to eat her Jersey potatoes with just a fork, like Tiffany, and dunking her bread roll in tomato ketchup. 'Yes. I made six and put strawberry jam in them. I'm going to take them *all* home.' Cassie put enough emphasis on the 'all' to forestall anyone even considering asking for one.

Unexpectedly Caroline smiled. 'I used to make jam tarts with Leo when he was little. Grace used to help us cook them.'

'Grace doesn't like you,' Cassie said matter-of-factly.

Alice cringed internally and held her breath, but Caroline took the blunt remark in her stride. 'Yes, I know. She loves Leo and she didn't like me taking him away. But he's back again now.'

146

'So Grace will like you again.' Cassie went back to her potatoes contentedly. She was rapidly getting the hang of holding her fork in her right hand, and Alice could foresee a problem arising when the little girl next ate a meal at home.

'It would be nice if that could happen,' Caroline said wistfully. 'I begged her to come with me, didn't I, Peter? But she wouldn't leave you. She was too damned loyal.'

'You said a naughty word,' Cassie said reprovingly and Alice decided quickly that it was time to take her niece home.

'We'd better go, I think,' she said firmly. Any moment now Cassie would insist that Caroline sat on the naughty stair.

They had to collect the jam tarts from the kitchen before they left and Leo caught up with them outside the kitchen door.

'I need to talk to you.'

Alice smiled at Cassie. 'You go and

147

find Grace and collect your tarts. I won't be a minute.' She looked at Leo. 'I'll be here tomorrow — can't it wait until then?'

'I may have to go to the hospital with Tiffany tomorrow, that's what I wanted to explain.'

'So you won't need me?'

'That's the problem, Alice. I'm beginning to need you more and more, and I don't know what to do about it.' He gave her a baffled look. 'This is ridiculous. That sounded like some really bad dialogue from one of my books.'

'Don't worry. I can always edit it out.' She gave him a tentative little smile. She had no idea where he was going with this. He would be leaving soon. Needing her wasn't an option.

At that moment Cassie came out of the kitchen carrying a plate of tarts. 'You look like the Queen of Hearts, Cassie. Say goodbye to Leo — we have to go home.'

At the front door Cassie blew Leo a

kiss. 'Mummy says if you sniff it up your nose it stays with you for ever.'

Alice shrugged apologetically. 'I have a weird sister.'

He ruffled Cassie's hair. 'She sounds like fun. I'll have to meet her one day.'

And what would Lauren make of Leo? Alice wondered if she would ever find out.

8

The boiler repair company's van was outside the house when Alice drove up, and she felt a panic attack coming on. If the boiler had packed up for good, they were in trouble. Leo hadn't paid her yet and she didn't want to have to beg for an advance. She helped Cassie out of the car, hoping fervently that things weren't as bad as they looked.

She unlocked the door, letting Cassie run in ahead of her. Lauren was sitting at the kitchen table, an empty mug in front of her, while the person leaning nonchalantly against the sink was likely to be the new boiler man.

'What's wrong?' she asked anxiously. 'Has it given up the ghost for good?'

Cassie was pulling at her mother's sleeve asking for a plate for her tarts and Lauren looked at Alice blankly. 'Has what given up what?'

'The boiler.' She looked at the man by the sink, taking in the fact that he was far better-looking than most boiler men. 'Has it packed up for good?'

'Ah, the boiler.' He was tall and dark and definitely on the handsome side, even if he didn't have Leo's golden perfection. 'The boiler's holding up quite well, actually.' He gave her a grin that showed a good set of white teeth. 'I didn't call about the boiler. I came to ask Lauren out.'

It took a lot to fluster Lauren, but she was definitely flustered now. Her face was pink and she clearly didn't know what to do with her hands.

Alice watched her with amusement, then came to her sister's rescue. 'Do you want to go out with this man?'

'If you can babysit tonight.'

'I'm not a baby.' Cassie looked at her mother reproachfully. 'Why did you just call me a baby? I'm nearly six — and I made jam tarts.'

'I'm sorry, Cassie. This is Joe. Perhaps he'd like to try one of your tarts.'

Somewhat mollified, Cassie put a particularly sticky-looking jam tart in Joe's hand. 'Are you another prince, or just a knight?' she demanded.

'Oh, definitely just a knight,' he told her with a smile. 'I rescue ladies in distress.'

Alice was having trouble visualising Lauren on a date, and she couldn't imagine why. Michael had been gone for over five years and it was time Lauren dated again. So why was the idea making her feel abandoned? She should be happy for her sister.

'Of course I'll look after Cassie. I can put her to bed if you like. What time do you want to leave?'

'Seven-thirty would be about right,' Joe said. 'I've got another call, so I'll be off now. Nice meeting you all.'

Alice watched him leave. The old boiler man used to wear overalls, but Joe looked pretty good in black jeans and a T-shirt. Perhaps modern boilers weren't as dirty as they used to be.

'Nice work, sister,' she remarked. 'It's

about time you started having some fun.'

★   ★   ★

Lauren started getting ready for her date as soon as Joe left. 'I didn't ask where we're going, so I have no idea what to wear. It could be anything from jeans at a burger bar to a posh frock at one of those fusion restaurants.' She spun round with a pair of shoes in each hand. 'Heels or flats?' She let out a wail. 'I can't do this, Alice. I should have told him I can't go.'

'You have hours before Joe picks you up. Lay everything out on the bed and then pick something that will look good anywhere. How about that grey skirt you got in the sale, teamed up with a pretty top and heels? You need to dress up a little bit, even if he does take you to McDonalds. It's still a date.'

'Can't I take you with me? I'm no good at things like this on my own.'

Alice laughed sympathetically. 'Sorry,

sister. If I come with you tonight I'll have to bring Cassie with me, and then it really will be McDonalds.'

Cassie was in bed but not asleep when Joe arrived and he went upstairs with Lauren to say goodnight. The child seemed more excited than her mother. The knight might not be wearing shining armour, but that didn't matter to Cassie. He had to answer a couple of questions, like where he'd left his horse and what he had done with his sword, but he handled the interrogation quite well and went up in Alice's estimation.

★   ★   ★

Half an hour later, Lauren and Joe had left and Cassie was asleep. Alice stretched out on the sofa, missing her sister already. Sometimes they got a babysitter and went to see a movie, or had a meal out, but always together. Since their mother died they had hardly been apart.

Lauren occasionally attended a con-ference to do with hair styling, and sometimes Alice went on a school field trip, but they were never away from one another for long. Alice hadn't allowed herself to think that Lauren might one day meet someone important enough to make her leave for good; there was no point in worrying about things before they happened.

But now Lauren had a date.

Restless, Alice looked at her watch. It was still early. They would barely have started their first course. Lauren wouldn't be home for a long time yet.

It was time to get over herself and watch a movie. She kicked off her shoes, put her feet up on the sofa, and was just beginning to understand the plot of a rather convoluted thriller, when the doorbell rang.

Not Lauren, surely! Had something gone wrong? Everything from a car accident to an attack by the boiler man went through Alice's head as she warily opened the front door.

Leo looked at her apprehensively. 'Is this a bad time? You look worried.'

'No. I thought you might be my sister. She's out on a date.'

'I see,' he said, not seeing at all. 'If you're on your own, can I come in? Like I said before, I really need to talk to you.'

She moved out of the way and he walked past her into the living room.

'Nice,' he said approvingly, dropping down onto the sofa. 'Comfortable.'

If he meant a bit untidy, he was probably right. Magazines were scattered over the coffee table and a couple of Cassie's dolls lay on the floor. Alice picked them up hastily, wondering what on earth Leo wanted to talk about. Something important enough to warrant a visit must be bordering on a crisis. Perhaps her editing was so appalling that he was going to sack her without pay.

'Why are you here, Leo? It must be something important.'

'It is. Well, I think it is. But, first of all, I want to let you know I shall need you tomorrow — that is, if you haven't already made other plans. Tiffany doesn't want me to go to the hospital with her. Dad's going to take her and my mother is going with them.'

He ran a hand through his hair. 'Please sit down, Alice — you're making me nervous, standing over me like that.'

She hesitated. Should she sit next to him, or on the other side of the room? In the end, she sat beside him. It was a fairly big sofa.

'I shall have to bring Cassie with me tomorrow,' she said apologetically. 'I haven't got anything planned, but Lauren booked in a couple of colouring sessions because she thought I'd be here all day.'

'Cassie is welcome any time, you know that. Grace loves to fuss over her.'

'Would you like a drink?' Alice asked when the silence had stretched a bit too far. 'We have white wine, or I can make you a cup of tea.'

'Tea would be great. I'm getting quite a taste for it. I suppose I must have drunk it when I lived here before, but I don't remember.' He followed her into the kitchen and waited while she filled the kettle. 'I expect you're wondering why Tiff has to make a hospital visit. All the secrecy is ridiculous. It must seem as if we're all deliberately keeping secrets from you.'

'A family is entitled to secrets, Leo. I don't need to know your business. I just work for you.' She took a bottle of milk from the fridge. 'We actually have enough milk tonight, so I won't need to run to the store in my pyjamas.'

'Which is a great pity. I'll always remember that night with pleasure.' He added sugar to his mug of tea. 'Tiffany's diabetes has caused trouble with her eyes and she needs an operation.'

He was right behind Alice when she walked back into the living room. 'She could have had the same op in LA, or gone to some other private hospital, but my father is one of the best eye surgeons in the world. Tiffany is his step-daughter and he's never met her, so I suggested we take a short vacation over here and let him do the operation.'

He sat down on the sofa and took a sip of his tea. 'Dad was brilliant about it, but then my mother found out what we were planning and suddenly everything changed.'

'I suppose she doesn't want Dr Grant to do the operation?' Alice could see why. She supposed it had put the poor woman in an impossible situation.

'You're right.' Leo sighed. 'That was the last thing she wanted. She showed Tiff brochures from about twenty alternative eye hospitals dotted all over the States. As far as she was concerned, anything would be better than putting her precious daughter's sight in the hands of my dad, however capable he was. But Tiffany put her foot down. She wanted the operation done over here because there was less chance of the agency finding out.'

Alice was silent for a few minutes, sipping her tea. So that was why Tiffany always wore tinted spectacles or sunglasses.

'Is the operation for cataracts? I thought that was a fairly simple procedure.'

Leo shook his head. 'Unfortunately, no. I wish that was all it was. Tiff was stupid enough to ignore the problems with her vision until she could hardly see. Dad had to do loads of tests because an operation at this late stage can be quite risky. She goes for her final assessment tomorrow and he has her booked in for next week.'

'We should have finished the editing before then,' Alice said. 'So you can be at the hospital when she needs you.'

'I should have noticed there was something wrong when she came back from working in Milan and asked if she could move in with me,' Leo went on, as if to himself. 'Her sight was so bad by then, she was scared of being on her own. I was right in the middle of the book and she was being a damned nuisance, much more clingy than usual.

I very nearly kicked her out.'

And you're still feeling guilty about that, Alice thought.

'But then she told you?'

'Yeah. And then I spent a long time kicking myself. Dad has been great, organising all this. He won't let Tiff pay for the operation, even though she can afford it, and we've really disrupted his life.'

Alice smiled. 'I think he's secretly enjoying every minute of it. Mind you, he may not enjoy being reunited with Caroline quite as much. She's a strong lady.'

'She absolutely adores Tiffany, but there seems to be a problem with mothers and teenage daughters. One of them always has to win.'

'And there's likely to be more of a problem between a wife and her ex-husband.' Alice grimaced. 'I wish you luck.'

'So I guess you'll be glad when your editing job is finished.'

It wasn't a question, but Alice sensed

something behind his casual words. 'Not really.' she turned to look at him. 'I'm enjoying it.' She hesitated, burning boats coming to mind. 'And I enjoy working for you.'

'Seriously?' He moved nearer to her on the sofa. 'Will you miss me when I'm gone?'

He should have said it flippantly, but he didn't. It was a serious question. She could see that in his eyes.

'Yes,' she answered, just as seriously. 'I'm beginning to wish I hadn't met you, Leo. You're going to be hard to forget.'

'It might be an idea — ' his hip was touching hers now — 'if we make the most of the time we have left. You owe me a kiss, at the very least.'

It was very easy to slip into his arms. She told herself it didn't matter because soon he would be gone, and it was just a kiss.

But it wasn't just a kiss.

She found that out as soon as his lips touched hers. Sleeping Beauty wouldn't have stood a chance. If Alice could have moved closer, she would have done, but other than crawl on to his lap, she was as close as she could get. She moaned against his mouth as his arms tightened round her — there was no gear lever this time to get in his way . . . and then she heard footsteps on the stairs.

Cassie! She pulled away from him, pressing her hands against his chest to make him release her, straightening her clothes as the door opened.

Cassie stood blinking in the light. 'Is Mummy home yet?' She saw Leo and gave him a sleepy smile. 'Hello, Mister Leo. Are you having a sleepover with Aunty Alice?'

Leo's laughter broke the spell and Alice found herself laughing as well. Out of the mouths of babes.

'Not tonight, sweetheart,' Leo said, 'but some other time, perhaps. Did you come downstairs for milk and cookies? I find hot milk helps me sleep.' He patted the sofa beside him. 'Come and sit with me while your aunty gets you a drink.'

'No cookies, it's too late, but I'll get you a drink of milk if you promise me you'll go straight back to bed.'

Alice walked into the kitchen thanking her lucky stars she had heard Cassie on the stairs. If the little girl had walked in a few seconds earlier, there would have been a lot of explaining to do.

Mind you, she thought with a smile as she heated a mug of milk in the microwave, *a few seconds later and an explanation might not have been possible.* She stirred the milk to make sure it wasn't too hot and carried it back into the room.

Cassie cuddled up between them and Leo told her a story about an ogre who kept a princess locked in his castle until a prince rescued her. Then he had to re-tell it to include a knight.

Alice tried to explain. 'Lauren's on a date with a boiler repair man called Joe, and because you're Cassie's prince, Joe has to be a knight. Does that make any sense at all? We all belong in her fairy story one way or another.'

'It makes perfect sense. I was brought up on fairy stories. My father has all the best books, Hans Christian Andersen, The Brothers Grimm, *Peter Pan, The Water Babies.* Even though some of his books are rare copies, he always let my mother read them to me. If she was out, which she was quite a lot, Grace used to read to me instead.'

He took Cassie's mug out of her hand before she dropped it. She was nearly asleep beside him. 'I still have a princess to rescue somewhere.'

'Well, I must put Sleeping Beauty back to bed before her mother comes home, and it might be a good idea if you're gone before then as well — or I shall be up all night explaining everything to my nosy sister.'

She walked with him to the front door, backing away determinedly when he tried to kiss her goodnight. 'Go home, Leo. I'll see you in the morning.'

She pulled open the front door to let him out, and Lauren almost fell in. She must have been leaning against the door jamb. Joe, just behind her, looked startled.

'I was just about to put my key in the lock,' Lauren said, although there was no sign of a key in her hand. She suddenly noticed Leo. 'You're Leo Grant, aren't you? Your picture was all over the village last week.'

'And you must be Lauren. I've been wanting to meet you.'

Now Lauren did look flustered and Alice was beginning to feel the same way. What do you do with two good-looking men on your doorstep late at night? As it was, she didn't have to solve the problem. Cassie did it for her.

'Mummy, Mummy, Mummy! You're home. Did you have a nice time? I had warm milk and Mister Leo told me a story about a princess. Can I stay up a bit longer?'

'No way, princess. Off to bed with you, I'll be up in a minute.' Lauren looked at Joe. 'I have to go and get my daughter back to bed — but thank you for a lovely evening.'

'I must leave as well,' Leo said. He noticed Joe's car, a racy little sports number in bright red. 'Nice wheels. I've had to make do with a hire-car since I've been over here.'

'I've only had it a few weeks, but it goes like a bomb. Do you want to come and have a look?'

As the two men walked towards their cars, Alice closed the front door with a deep sigh of relief. 'I can only cope with one man at a time.'

'You only have to cope with one. The other one's mine.'

Alice laughed. 'I take it he lived up to expectations.'

'More than.' Lauren sighed. 'He's really nice. I thought I'd be going to the restaurant in his van, and that would have been fine, but that little car is amazing, and he's so thrilled with it.

'His dad died some months ago and he inherited the business. He's not really a repair man, he's a design engineer for a plumbing and heating company, but he needs to keep his dad's business going until he can get someone in to run it for him.' Lauren started up the stairs. 'Has Cassie been a pain?' she called over her shoulder.

'She heard Leo's voice, I think. That's what brought her downstairs. I warmed some milk for her and Leo told her a story. Go and get her settled, and then we can talk.'

★　★　★

Alice didn't tell Lauren about Leo's kiss and later, when she was in bed, she wondered why. Normally, the sisters told one another all their secrets, but the kiss was not for sharing. She knew she was being silly, letting Leo into her life, but she couldn't help it. She felt as if she was caught up in the middle of a fairy story that had to run its course, even though she doubted there would be a happy ending.

Lauren, on the other hand, wanted to share everything. 'He's too good to be true, isn't he? A really nice man with a good job who likes children. I don't meet people like that, do I?'

'Because you never go anywhere. You haven't been on a proper date since Michael died, and that was a long time ago. You deserve someone nice.'

'He wants to take me out again, me and Cassie — maybe at the weekend. You can come too, of course. I won't leave you alone at the weekend.'

Alice frowned. She was a young professional woman, not someone to be pitied, and if she didn't have a boyfriend herself, it was partly because she didn't like leaving Lauren on her own. Now the tables had turned and Alice knew she had to prove she was quite capable of managing on her own. Somewhere in the future, there had always been a scary scenario when one of them would be left alone. It was just her bad luck to meet someone like Leo and then find she was going to lose him.

She gave Lauren a hug. 'Thanks for

the offer, but I'm sure I'll find something to do. I'm not completely helpless. You and Cassie have a good time. It will be nice for the three of you to go out together.'

Lauren grinned. 'If Cassie takes a dislike to him, she'll tell him, won't she?'

'You can bet on it.'

9

Alice felt nervous the next morning as she parked outside the house. Cassie couldn't wait to get inside but Alice hung on to her niece's hand, needing protection from something she couldn't quite name. Grace met them at the door.

'We have a special lunch today,' she told the little girl. 'Pizza and ice cream.' Cassie whooped and the woman laughed. 'But first we have to make the pizza.'

'You don't have to make pizza,' Cassie was explaining as Grace took her hand and headed towards the kitchen. 'A man brings it in a box.'

Leo laughed beside her, making Alice jump. 'Cassie will learn a lot from Grace. I did.'

'How to make pizza?'

'Wasted effort. I know a man who'll

bring it in a box.'

'But I bet Grace's pizzas taste better.' She followed him into the library. 'Are those the books you were telling me about?' she asked, pointing to a row of books on the top shelf.

Leo swung the ladder across on its runners and climbed up to bring one down. He held out the ancient volume and she stared at the front cover. *Alice's Adventures in Wonderland*, by Lewis Carroll, with illustrations by John Tenniel. He flipped open a page showing a coloured picture of Alice with the Dodo.

'She doesn't look much like you, does she?'

'I'm glad. She's got a big head and a really grumpy expression. Besides, I never wear blue and white striped tights. Where's the Jabberwock?'

He studied a list of illustrations and found the page. 'I used to know the poem off by heart. I probably still do.'

She took the book from him and stared at the picture. The beast didn't look very dragon-like although it did have a long green neck and purple wings. 'Say it to me.'

He remembered every word and she stood spellbound.

'What's a vorpal blade?'

He waved an imaginary sword. 'I have no idea, but it sounds pretty fierce, doesn't it? I bet it would cut that critter's head off.'

'Snicker snack, like the poem says. You must ask your father if we can show this to Cassie. She'd just love it.'

Leo climbed the ladder to replace the book. 'All the best ones are up here,' he said, looking down at her. 'Dad wasn't trying to keep them out of my reach. He just needs his medical ones close to hand.' He held up another book. 'The *Water Babies*, with colour pictures by Warwick Goble. This book is probably a bit old for Cassie at the moment. I always felt it was written for grown-ups rather than children and found it very boring.' He put the book back and climbed down the ladder. 'But perhaps

I should read it again. From what I remember, it was quite political in places.'

'A lot of the old children's stories are really scary, even the fairy stories, but Cassie loves them. She seems quite capable of separating fact and fiction, although she lives in her own little dream world most of the time.' Alice glanced at the clock on the wall. 'We'd better get some work done.'

'You do realise,' he said slowly, 'we're all alone today. My father, mother, and sister are all in London.'

'But,' Alice moved smartly to the other side of the desk, 'Cassie is just down the hall. She nearly walked in on us last night and I won't let it happen again.'

'It was only a kiss, Alice. I doubt it would have traumatised Cassie for the rest of her life.'

Alice kept her head down while she sorted papers on the desk. The word 'only' had hurt her a little, but he was quite right — he didn't exactly force her into anything. He probably kissed all the girls that way. More fool her, for thinking it had been something special.

'Are you looking for something specific,' he asked, 'or just having a general shuffle around? Because you don't seem to be achieving much at the moment.'

She looked up to see barely hidden laughter in his eyes.

'I know what you're thinking, and you're wrong. It was never just a kiss, Alice. We both know that.'

He turned towards the window as a car door slammed outside. 'There's a taxi outside. It looks as if Tiffany and my mother are back. What on earth is going on?'

Alice followed him out into the hall just as the front door burst open. An angry Caroline stormed into the house, closely followed by Tiffany.

'I *said* we shouldn't trust him.' Caroline faced Leo, completely ignoring Alice. 'All that way for nothing. We waited ages at the hospital and then a nurse told us your father had been called to an emergency. Some silly child who fell off his bike. Surely Peter isn't the only surgeon in the world? We had a booked appointment.'

'Mom, a little boy was badly hurt,' Tiffany said tiredly. 'From what the nurse told us, he shattered his cheekbone on the sidewalk and could lose his eye. Dr Grant had to go see him.'

Caroline sat down on the stairs and kicked off her shoes. 'We had an appointment,' she repeated stubbornly.

'Dad's the best eye surgeon in the country, Mother,' Leo said quietly. 'If anyone can save the kid's eye, he can. Tiffany was only there for a few tests before her operation next week.' He looked at his sister. 'Couldn't you have waited?'

'They weren't sure how long the operation on the little kid would take and Mom didn't want to wait. She was starting to freak out.'

'I hate hospitals.' Caroline looked quite forlorn sitting on the stairs. 'I simply couldn't wait there for hours. They said they'd reschedule the tests.'

'There you go, then.' Leo looked up as Grace came lumbering out of the kitchen, followed by a rather nervous-looking Cassie. 'Hi, little one. Have you made your pizza yet?'

Cassie shook her head and moved closer to Alice. 'We made dough and now we have to cook tomatoes for sauce.'

She stared at Caroline and asked. 'Why are you cross?'

'Because I'm a silly old woman making a fuss about nothing.' Caroline patted the stair. 'Come and sit here and tell me about this dough you made. Is it like play-dough?'

Cassie giggled and squeezed in beside Caroline. 'No, you can't play with it. It's to eat. The pizza has tomato sauce and onions and pepper . . . ' She paused and looked towards Grace for help. 'Pepper — something that looks like a big sausage.'

'Pepperoni.' Grace glanced down at

Caroline with something that could have been compassion. 'I'll go and make tea. Unless you'd rather have a jug of Sangria. It's already made for lunch.'

Leo gave her a grateful smile. 'Sangria would be great, Grace, and some juice for Cassie. We'll have our drinks outside in the garden.'

★ ★ ★

The sun was bright on the little patio and the cushions on the wicker furniture were warm. Cassie sat beside Caroline without being asked to do so and Alice thought how empathic children could be. The little girl was comforting the woman, just by being there.

Alice took off her cardigan and felt the heat from the sun on her arms. Summer was at its height, and in a few days Leo would be gone. She watched him as he joked with his sister, his golden hair glinting. A true lion's mane.

His name suited him.

Tiffany looked particularly tense, her long legs crossed tightly at the ankle, her hands gripping the arms of her chair.

Caroline seemed incapable of helping, and Alice decided the mother was just as stressed-out as the daughter. She tuned in to the conversation and heard Caroline say perhaps it was time to think again about having the operation done in America.

'It's too late for that, Mom — it really is. Please don't start all over again. I've made up my mind, and Dr Grant is operating next week.'

'If he doesn't get called out to another emergency. He's taking this whole thing far too lightly, but who can blame him? You're not his daughter after all, Tiffany. He has no reason to put himself out for you. You're just another patient to him.'

Feeling the tension mounting again, Cassie slipped from her seat beside Caroline. 'Can I go and find Grace?'

'We'll come with you.' Leo took Cassie's hand and looked across at Alice. 'Coming?'

Gratefully, she fell into step beside him.

'Will Tiffany be all right?'

He smiled. 'Oh yes, she's used to it. It's not that my mother doesn't care — she cares too much. She's finds it easier to block bad things out. Pretend they don't exist and they'll go away. She didn't want to come to England, she told Tiff she wouldn't, but then her conscience got the better of her. Now she's here she wishes she were back home, away from all the hassle. She's not good at dealing with the bad things in life. She looks fully in control of her life, but really she's always one step away from a nervous breakdown.'

'Poor Caroline.' Alice spoke with genuine sympathy. She would have liked to ask more questions about his mother, but Grace came out of the kitchen pushing a trolley.

'Sangria, with olives and warm bread

straight from the oven. Hungry people are not happy people.' She held open the kitchen door. 'Show your aunty your pizza dough while I take the drinks into the garden.'

★   ★   ★

The kitchen was warm. A large pot simmered on the stove, smelling of tomatoes and herbs. Alice sniffed appreciatively. 'Home-made tomato sauce! I can't wait. Like Grace says, your mother needs to eat. She's too thin.'

'Nervous energy. She's always been like that, a miniature tornado.' He lifted a cloth that was laid across the top of a bowl. 'Is this yours, Cassie?'

She looked in the bowl and then back at Leo, wide-eyed. 'My ball of dough was only little, what made it grow?'

He smoothed the cloth back over the bowl. 'Magic. Grace is really a witch, but a nice white witch. She never puts a bad spell on anyone.'

Cassie pursed her lips thoughtfully. 'Could Grace make me grow big, like my dough?'

Alice laughed. 'Get out of that one, Leo Grant!'

'She's too clever by half.' He took Cassie's hand. 'How about we go and find some food? As you're so grown up, you can have some olive oil to dip your bread in.'

Cassie looked up at him, an expression of extreme distaste on her face. 'I don't like olives.'

'Then I promise you won't have to eat one, but Grace baked the bread specially, so you have to try that.'

By the time they walked out into the garden the argument seemed to be over, but both women still looked wound up. Perhaps the Sangria would help, Alice thought, as she cut a slice of bread and drizzled oil and balsamic vinegar into a small bowl. Leo sat down beside her.

'Can I share?'

She pushed the bowl towards him.

The tension still filled the air like an electric storm about to happen, and she felt sorry for Tiffany. The girl had enough to put up with already without a neurotic mother breathing down her neck all the time.

'If you'd like to take the opportunity to go to the shopping centre,' she suggested tentatively, 'I can take you both. That's if Leo can spare me for half an hour.'

'Can I stay here with Grace, Aunty Alice?' Cassie asked. 'I've got to finish my pizza.'

'If Grace doesn't mind having you.' She smiled as Cassie headed for the door. 'Just be careful of the hot stove.'

Tiffany looked pleadingly at her mother. 'Can we go to the mall, please? We can get a taxi back.'

'We've nothing else to do now,' Caroline said pointedly, 'so I suppose we might as well shop, although I can't imagine there will be anything worth buying in a local store. Thank you for your offer, Alice, it would be most helpful if you could take us. We can find our own way back.'

Leo looked worried. 'Just don't let Tiff out of your sight, mother. She can't see more than a few feet in front of her.'

'Oh, for goodness' sake, Leo, I'm not stupid.' Caroline put down her drink and headed for the door. 'I'd better go change my shoes if we're going to be walking round a mall.'

'Thank you, Alice,' Tiffany said gratefully as Caroline left the room. 'Mom loves shopping. It makes her happy.'

'I'm glad something does,' Leo said dryly. He gave Alice a crooked grin. 'You can see now why we both left home at an early age. Just stay close to her, Tiff. She won't remember to look after you, not if there's a bargain to be had.'

'I will, I promise.'

'Was it a silly suggestion?' Alice asked worriedly, as Tiffany went in search of her mother. 'Perhaps I should stay with them while they shop.'

Leo shook his head vehemently. 'No way. Piggy in the middle is not a fun game to play with those two.' He took her hand. 'Will you have lunch with me later?'

'Much later, then. I've just stuffed myself full of delicious home-made bread.'

'We'll take my rental, and when we've dropped them off we'll find a nice pub by a river somewhere. How does that sound?'

'It will be better if you drive,' Alice said. 'After all that Sangria I was afraid I might be over the limit.'

'That batch of Sangria was non-alcoholic. Grace thought we were going to work on the book.'

'We should, shouldn't we? I keep distracting you.'

Leo pushed the door shut and held it closed with one hand. The other he slipped round the back of her neck and gently touched his lips to hers. 'When you hear me complaining, that's when you have to stop distracting me.' He stepped back to pull the door open for Caroline. 'But sometimes a distraction is exactly what everyone needs.'

'Yes, thank you, Alice.' Caroline had changed into cut-off jeans with a simple white top, an outfit that made her look ten years younger. It was the little worry lines round her eyes that gave her age away. 'Tiffany is really traumatised over this operation, and cancelling her test was unforgivable. I don't know how Peter could be so heartless.'

'It was only a pre-op test, Mother. The operation will still go ahead as planned.' He walked out into the hall just as Tiffany came down the stairs. 'I'm driving you to the mall and taking Alice out to lunch after we've dropped you off. Cassie is staying with Grace.'

Caroline frowned, a thoughtful look on her face. 'Don't forget you'll be going back home in a couple of weeks, Leo.'

Leo smiled. 'A lot can happen in a couple of weeks, Mother.'

Caroline shrugged. 'I just thought it

would be best not to get involved. This is not your home, Leo. You live on the other side of the Atlantic.'

Alice bit her tongue. Whatever she said now would only make matters worse. When they reached Leo's car, Caroline climbed into the front seat and Alice smiled to herself. Whatever Caroline thought might be going on, she seemed determined to put a stop to it. Alice sighed as she sat down next to Tiffany in the back of the car. Chance would be a fine thing.

★ ★ ★

Leo pulled into a parking space outside the shopping centre and Caroline and Tiffany got out.

'Have you brought your American Express card, Mom?' Tiffany asked her mother. 'You might find you need it.'

Caroline looked at the names on the backs of the shops. 'I must say there are more outlets than I expected.' She watched Alice move to the front passenger seat beside Leo. 'I'll use my cell phone to call you when we're ready to leave. If you're both still out, you can pick us up.'

'I mustn't be too long,' Alice said a little worriedly. 'I don't want to take advantage of Grace. Cassie can be quite a handful at times.'

She wasn't prepared to admit that she was feeling a little nervous, now she was alone with Leo. Sitting next to him, she could smell his cologne; it was a heady mix of citrus and spice, but subtle enough to make her lean closer.

'That's nice,' she commented, 'what you're wearing. Did you buy it over here?'

He gave her a startled glance. 'My T-shirt? I've had it years.'

She laughed. 'No, your aftershave or cologne or whatever. It's not one I recognise.'

He negotiated a turn that led on to a country lane. 'Oh — it was a present. I can't remember what it's called. I'd have to look at the bottle.'

Alice remembered Caroline's words. This was not Leo's home. He had another life in America — and maybe a girlfriend who gave him cologne on his birthday.

'There's a wooded area a bit further along,' she said, recognising the area they were driving through. 'And if you keep going there's a village with a river and a pub. It's a bit pricey because of where it is, but really lovely from what I remember.'

'You've been here before with someone, have you?'

He said it casually, but she detected something in his voice that made her smile. Was it possible he was just as unsure of himself as she was?

Looking at his profile, she doubted it. He looked completely relaxed; one hand resting on the steering wheel, the other on the sill of the open window. The breeze was blowing his rippling hair across his face, and she fought the urge to reach over and brush the gold-tipped curls out of his eyes.

He really was quite beautiful.

Instead, she reached up and pushed the button to open the sunroof. 'Close your window, and then you'll be able to see where you're going,' she admonished. 'Didn't anyone ever make you get your hair cut when you were a boy? It's positively dangerous like that.'

He turned his head long enough to give her a brief grin. 'Yes, they did. Grace was always nagging me and my father said I looked like a girl. I had to do what I was told then — but not any more. Now I can do what I like.' He closed his window. 'Don't you like my surfer look?'

'Oh, is that what it is? I thought for a moment you were just too lazy to go to a hairdresser.' She touched his arm and pointed to a road sign. 'There — The Swan. That's the pub I was talking about.'

He slowed for the turning. 'A very original name. I imagine there are swans on a river somewhere nearby.'

She smiled as the road skirted the

village green. 'If I remember rightly, there's a garden at the back leading down to the river and, yes, there are swans. Is it warm enough today to eat outside, do you think?'

He parked and opened the car door. 'Definitely warm enough. Are you hungry again now?'

'A beer would be nice to start with.'

She followed him through the bar to the decking outside and grabbed a table that had just become vacant. 'I should imagine it's difficult to get a seat out here if the weather's good.' She pointed. 'And — look! — there are your swans.'

Two of the elegant creatures floated by on water that was so clear Alice could see their orange feet paddling lazily below the surface. She looked at Leo and felt one of those rare moments of blissful happiness. Whatever happened in a few days' time, she would always have this moment with him to treasure.

She came out of her reverie to find

him smiling at her.

'Where were you, Alice?' he asked. 'Back in Cassie's world of make-believe? I don't blame you. This place is like something out of a fairy story. A perfect English pub in a perfect English village. I wish I could bottle it and take it back home with me.'

'I was day-dreaming,' she said, her moment of euphoria fading with his words. She needed his reminder that this was all temporary. Just a rather beautiful dream. There was no Prince Charming or knight in shining armour to whisk her away to a fairytale land.

Soon he would be gone, and all she would have left were these few precious moments.

'How about that beer?' she asked.

10

Leo still wasn't feeling hungry and when he asked Alice if she wanted him to order some food, she shook her head.

'Too much bread earlier, and I need to walk off the beer. Let's go for a stroll along the riverbank while the sun's out.'

He took her hand and she let him. When they reached a little bridge that crossed the river, he dropped down onto the grassy bank and pulled her down to sit beside him.

'These are the little white flowers for making chains,' he said. 'I remember my mother showing me how. She'd had a row with my father because he was going away again and she took me for a walk. I must have been about four years old.'

He picked a daisy and scored the stem with his thumbnail, slotting the next one through. When he had a small ring of the white flowers, he set them on her head like a crown.

'Now you're a real princess.'

She laughed up at him and he bent his head to kiss her. He had intended the kiss to be a light touch of his lips on hers, but something happened in that small moment of time and the kiss turned into something else entirely.

When, pulse pounding, he eventually let her go, he knew with absolute certainty that he wanted her to stay in his life. He cupped her chin and looked deep into her eyes.

'What are we going to do about us, Alice?'

'Us? There isn't any us. You're going back to America.'

'But there could be, couldn't there? I've only just met you, but I can't let you slip away from me. I want time to get to know you.' He caught both her hands in his. 'Come back with me when I leave next week. Let me show you my world.'

He watched her face intently and saw hope flare like a ray of sunshine, but then reality dimmed the light in her eyes.

'I have obligations here, Leo. I can't drop everything at a moment's notice and fly across the Atlantic with you.' She took a breath. 'You could stay here, though. You were born here, your father still lives here. And you can write anywhere.'

He got to his feet and stared at the river. What obligations did he have? Whether the operation was a success or not, Tiffany had to learn how to look after herself. Perhaps he was a hindrance rather than a help; simply a crutch she must learn to do without.

'I've never really thought about moving back to England. Not permanently, anyway.' He held out his hand and helped Alice to her feet. 'It would take a while to sort things out over there, but it could be done.'

He saw the look of doubt on her face. 'You'd really stay here? In England? For me?'

Very gently, he slid his arms round her waist and pulled her towards him until their bodies were touching.

'I think I might.'

She must have been holding her breath because it came out in a little sigh. 'What if you get to know me and find you don't like me?'

'Then I'll go back to America and spend the rest of my miserable life trying to forget you.'

That made her laugh. She disentangled herself from his arms. 'You have a whole week to change your mind.'

'And only one week to find out if I really like you. That might not be long enough. It will probably take a lot of time and effort before I make up my mind. I think I like kissing you, but I need to be certain . . . '

His phone started ringing and he took it out with a curse. Perfect timing, as usual. He looked at the screen. 'It's my mother. I didn't expect them to finish shopping this early.'

He saw Alice watching his face as he

listened. Caroline sounded hysterical and he couldn't understand what she was saying. He tried to get her to talk more slowly but it took him a minute before he realised something was wrong.

'I don't understand. How *could* you lose her? You promised to look after her.' Still holding the phone to his ear, he looked at Alice, unable to hide his anger. 'I don't care. It doesn't matter now, does it? Look, stay where you are. Don't move an inch unless you see her. Running around in circles isn't going to help. We'll be with you in twenty minutes.'

'What's happened?' Alice asked, genuinely concerned.

He caught her hand, pulling her after him. He didn't have time to be gentle. 'Tiffany's gone missing. We have to hurry.' He thought of Tiffany, half-blind, wandering alone in the shopping centre. Once she lost sight of her mother, she wouldn't know how to find her again.

The basic rental car handled well when he put his foot down. The country lanes were narrow in places and he had to keep reminding himself which side of the road to drive on, but they made it in one piece — and in just sixteen minutes. He threw the car into the first available space and started towards the entrance without waiting for Alice.

His mother was standing where he had told her to wait. Her face was pale under her make-up and she twisted her hands together as if she didn't quite know what to do with them.

'She deliberately lost me. I told her to keep close.'

'I thought you said *you* lost *her*.' He was having trouble hiding his anger, but losing his temper wasn't going to help. 'You can't blame Tiff. If you move out of her range of vision, she can't see you. You needed to keep her close.' He forced himself to take a breath, scanning the crowd with anguished eyes. 'Never mind. Just tell me what happened. Where exactly were you when you lost her?'

'I didn't . . . ' Caroline began, but then she saw the expression on his face and started again. 'We were in the purse shop. The one behind me. At first I ran around looking for her, but then I thought she might ask someone where the shop was, so I came back here. When she still wasn't here, I didn't know what to do, so I phoned you.'

Alice put her hand gently on Caroline's arm. 'Have you spoken to anyone here? They have a speaker system for lost children and they'll send security staff to try and find her. Do you want me to do that?'

'Please.' Leo looked at Alice distractedly; he had almost forgotten she was there. 'If my mother stays here in case Tiff finds her way back, I'll look around the immediate area, but I agree we can't cover the whole store ourselves. We're going to need help.'

He felt frustrated at his impotence.

He wanted to do exactly what he had told his mother not to do — go rushing around, calling Tiffany's name. He watched Alice disappear towards the enquiries desk. Right at this moment, he couldn't worry about her as well. She could see the way to go; his sister couldn't.

He knew he shouldn't have trusted his mother to take care of Tiffany. He couldn't trust anyone except himself. He could feel the full weight of his burden slip back onto his shoulders again. His sister would always be his responsibility, and anything else was just a remote dream.

He had no idea in which direction to start looking. People were moving constantly. He could only rely on his height to see over the milling shoppers and hopefully spot Tiffany's red hair.

Once he thought he glimpsed her, but when he ran, calling her name and jostling people in his haste, it turned out to be another tall girl with red hair who looked thoroughly alarmed when he ran towards her. Not Tiffany.

They rendezvoused back at the handbag shop. The security team had left instructions with staff manning the three main exits and taken a detailed description. Leo could think of no reason Tiffany would leave the mall, but every conceivable eventuality had to be covered. Alice phoned the local police, but they didn't show much interest in an eighteen-year-old girl missing in a shopping mall. Leo had to admit the police would probably have laughed at him in LA if he had gone to them with the same problem.

Eventually, he told Alice to go back to his father's house and collect Cassie.

'You have to go and get her. She'll be wondering where you are and her mother will worry if you're late.' He took her hand, wishing he could go back a couple of hours to a time when he was considering changing his life for her. Now his perspective had shifted again, and if he were forced to make a choice, he would put his sister first as always. 'I'll keep you informed.'

'I'll get a taxi back to the house and pick up my car. Don't put all the blame on your mother, Leo. Tiffany may have gone to look at something and got turned around. It's difficult to watch someone all the time in this sort of environment.'

He didn't need Alice's advice. His mother had promised to look after Tiffany, and there was no excuse he could think off that would let her off that particular hook.

'We came here with Tiff a couple of days ago and we managed to keep her safe,' he said gruffly. 'Go home, Alice. This is not your problem.'

He turned to watch her disappear into the crowd. Now he didn't have Alice as a distraction, he could concentrate on finding his sister.

* * *

Alice collected Cassie from a worried Grace and explained what had happened as best she could.

'That woman, she cannot look after her own daughter,' Grace growled. 'She's not a good mother. She never looked after Leo and then she took him away. The girl is far too young to be a model and go to other countries on her own. A good mother would know that.'

Alice noticed Grace's accent got stronger when she was stressed. 'I think Caroline does what she can. Not everyone knows how to be a good mother, they just have to do their best.'

'What happened to Tiffany?' Cassie asked. 'Is she really lost? Perhaps the dragon locked her in a tower.'

'Perhaps he did, but the prince will rescue her. Now we have to get you home and let your mummy know what's happened. She'll be worrying about you.'

Alice had already made a quick phone call to Lauren before she called the taxi. Now she thanked Grace for looking after Cassie and drove home as quickly as she could. She brought

Lauren up to date and then phoned Leo.

'No, no news. She's still missing.' Alice could hear the frustration in his voice. 'You could walk round this place for hours and not meet the same person twice. Did you know it has three levels?'

Alice couldn't think of any reason why Tiffany, with her restricted vision, would have gone up to a floor that meant navigating a moving staircase or a lift.

Unless she didn't want to be found.

Keeping her thoughts to herself, Alice asked if she could come back and help him look, three pairs of eyes being better than two, but he told her to stay at home. Everything that could be done was being done, and he and his mother would stay until closing time, which was eight o'clock.

Alice reluctantly agreed, telling him to keep in touch. She could feel him moving away from her. She wasn't part of his family and he was now totally focused on finding his sister. At that precise moment he had no time for her, and she would only get in his way.

Cassie announced with absolute certainty that Tiffany would be rescued, safe and sound, and they had nothing to worry about. Lauren was bustling about in the kitchen.

'I asked Joe round for a meal — I thought it would be nice for you to get to know him a bit better — but if this is a really bad time, I can put him off.'

'No.' Alice shook her head. 'No, it's a good idea. He'll be a nice distraction from all the angst over at Breakwater. I offered to go back and help look, but Leo doesn't want me there.'

'I expect he's too worried to think straight. Besides, he's got his mother to cope with as well. Give him a bit of slack.'

'We went for a walk and he made me a daisy chain. He said he wanted to get to know me better and he was thinking about staying in England for good.' Alice sighed. 'Now all he can think about is his sister. Whenever he tries to do something with his life, she messes up and he has to sort her out.'

'Do you think she does it deliberately? To attract attention?'

'No, I don't think so, although she relies on him too much. Maybe when she can see properly again, she won't be so dependant on him.'

'I wouldn't bank on it. What she needs is a man in her life — then she'll dump her beloved brother so quickly he won't know what's happened.'

'I don't think that would break his heart. He thought she was off his hands for good when she went to Milan, but then she messed up her diabetes regime and finished up in hospital. I doubt she does it deliberately, though. Getting signed up with a big agency was just too much too soon, like some of the young rock stars who go to pieces after a few months. All the glitz and glamour goes to their head and they can't cope. Now Tiffany's gone and got lost in a shopping precinct.'

Lauren set out place mats on the

kitchen table. 'I don't understand how anyone could go missing for that length of time at Breakwater unless they didn't want to be found. The girl may not be able to see very well, but she's got a tongue in her head, hasn't she? Surely she would have the sense to ask where the handbag shop was, or even ask someone to take her to the information centre. They would have put a message out asking her mother to come and get her, in the same way that they would with a lost child.'

At that moment the doorbell rang and Lauren looked anxiously at Alice. 'Are you absolutely sure you don't mind Joe coming over?'

Alice laughed. 'Oh, for goodness' sake let him in, Lauren. It's been a long day and I need something to cheer me up.'

Joe walked in looking just as worried as Lauren.

'I hope this isn't a bad time,' he said anxiously.

He was wearing tight black jeans with

a short-sleeved shirt, a gold watch glinting on a wrist covered in short dark hair. Alice thought he looked pretty good and smiled at her sister.

'I'll take Cassie upstairs and get her changed into something clean. I have no idea what she's been up to with Grace. There's nothing more I can do to help find Tiffany,' she told Joe. 'I was more or less told that it's a family problem and none of my business anyway.'

Joe settled himself at the kitchen table. 'She's a grown-up. She should have been found by now. Hasn't she got some sort of tricky operation coming up? I reckon she's done a runner.'

Lauren raised her hands. 'I said exactly the same. She's gone missing on purpose.'

Alice had to admit the same thought had crossed her mind. 'But Tiffany doesn't know anyone here. Where would she go?'

Joe grinned. 'Somewhere to change her name, I shouldn't wonder. Who lumbered the poor kid with a name like Tiffany?'

'She's American,' Lauren said, as if that explained everything.

Alice shooed Cassie in front of her and headed up the stairs. Joe was the perfect match for Lauren. Funny and down-to-earth, besides being particularly good to look at. He was definitely taking her mind off missing teenagers.

By the time they came downstairs again Lauren had put homemade cheese straws on a plate and was sitting next to Joe. 'My daughter was missing today as well, so I had time to bake. There's a chocolate cake in the fridge for afters.'

Alice tried to keep her mind off anything that might be happening at Breakwater but she found she kept looking at her watch. Eight o'clock was the deadline. If Tiffany hadn't been found by the time the place closed down, she didn't know what Leo would do. If the girl wasn't at the shopping centre, where could she be?

Dinner was a delicious chicken casserole with new potatoes and green beans. By the time they had eaten, Cassie's eyes were closing and Lauren took her up to bed. Alice found a fresh carton of cream in the fridge and made real coffee. She asked Joe how he was getting on with his job as a boiler repairman.

'Learning as I go,' he said with a laugh. 'I always thought design was the hard part but, goodness, how wrong I was. I've got aches and pains in places I didn't know I had. The house builders these days hide all the pipes away and don't leave a map. Sometimes it takes ages just to find a leaky valve.'

Lauren appeared with a smile on her face. 'She was asleep before I finished the first bedtime story. I don't know what Grace does with her all day, but it certainly works.' She sank down on the sofa next to Joe and linked her hand in his. 'Are you boring my sister with shop-talk?'

'Just trying to take her mind off the missing model.'

'You're sure she doesn't know anyone here?' Lauren asked.

Alice slowly shook her head. 'Not as far as I know. But, hang on — I'm sure she mentioned something once about having friends here in England.'

Lauren looked puzzled. 'But I thought you said she'd never been to Britain before.'

'Facebook! I just remembered. Tiffany said she had lots of friends on Facebook.'

'That's it, then.' Joe put down his coffee mug. 'Who's got a computer? We should be able to find out who her friends are and if anyone lives near enough for her to visit.'

'She might not be able to find her way around very well on foot,' Alice said, 'but she knows how to call a taxi. She's certainly used to that.'

Lauren came back into the kitchen carrying her laptop and put it down on the table. 'I've got a Facebook account. Hang on while I log in.'

Alice pulled up a chair next to Joe so

they were all on the same side of the table. It only took Lauren a minute to log in to her Facebook account. She clicked on 'search'.

'What's her last name?'

Alice shook her head, her heart plummeting. 'I don't know.' Were they going to be defeated before they'd even begun?

'I don't think her mother got married again but Tiffany might use her father's name, or she might use the name Grant.'

'Not to worry,' Lauren said cheerfully. 'There can't be many Tiffanys, surely.'

There were hundreds of them. Lauren started to scroll through the faces, but Joe stopped her.

'It might be quicker to Google her first. If she's a model, her name will be on Google somewhere.'

And it was. Tiffany had quite a number of mentions, including names of designers she had modelled for and the agency she was currently with. But none mentioned her last name.

Alice clapped a hand to her head. 'What is the matter with me? I don't want to bother Leo because he's got enough to cope with, and all this may come to nothing — but Grace will know Tiffany's surname. Grace knows everything about the family.'

'Grant,' Grace answered when Alice phoned the house. 'What else would she be called? Have they found her?'

'No,' Alice told her, 'but we're still trying. You've been a big help, Grace. Thanks.'

Tiffany Grant helped thin the Facebook pictures out a little, but it was a common name and not everyone had a picture.

Alice was sure Tiffany would have her face on the social networking site, though. It was all good publicity, particularly if you were a beautiful redhead trying to make a name for yourself as an international model.

'Bingo!' she cried, as Joe scrolled down the second page. 'The one with the bright red hair.'

Joe whistled through his teeth. 'How could you lose something like that?'

Lauren put a hand over his eyes. 'That's quite enough looking. Make yourself useful and find out who her friends are.'

Tiffany had hundreds of friends, but only a few in England. 'That one,' Joe said. 'Emily Stapleford. Look, she's right here in town. We're not going to be able to access her address, though, so what do we do now?'

Lauren stood up and pulled a telephone directory down from a shelf. 'If she's not ex-directory she'll be in here.'

Joe patted her on the bottom. 'You are so clever sometimes, Lauren, my love.'

Lauren narrowed her eyes at him before she started to riffle through the pages. 'There aren't that many Staplefords, not locally, anyway, and there aren't any at all with the initial E.'

'The directory entry is probably in

her father's name. We'll have to try them all.'

And that's what they did. Alice thought it would be better if she made the calls, and the fourth number came up trumps. She asked the man who answered whether Emily was home and was told to hang on a minute.

'Emily speaking.'

'Is Tiffany with you?' Alice asked.

'Who wants to know?' The girl's voice sounded very young and very wary.

'Tell Tiffany it's Alice. I only want to talk to her. I'm not with Leo or her mother, they're still at Breakwater.'

'She doesn't want to talk to anyone. She's not feeling well.'

'Please ask her to speak to me. I just want to make sure that she's okay.'

After a few minutes of whispering in the background, Tiffany said defiantly, 'I'm not coming back.'

'You don't have to,' Alice answered soothingly. 'But Leo is worried sick about you. He's always looked after you and he still feels responsible for you. He doesn't know if you're alive or dead, Tiffany. You're not being fair to him.'

'Okay, then you can tell him I'm fine. But I won't come back.'

'You can't stay away for ever.' There was silence on the other end of the line and Alice asked gently, 'Why did you run away?'

'I didn't run away. I just wanted time to think. Mom said the operation could be dangerous and I didn't know that. She doesn't think I need it. She said I could go completely blind if something goes wrong.'

Alice tried to work out what to say next. She was out of her depth here. 'How long are you going to stay with your friend?'

'They don't have room for me to stay overnight, but Emily recommended a good hotel. Leo doesn't have to worry about me. I can manage just fine.'

'But we have plenty of room here,' Alice said impulsively. 'Let me come and get you. I promise I won't tell Leo or your mother where you are. You know you can trust me.'

The silence lasted almost too long.

'Do you have the address?' Tiffany said at last.

Alice glanced at the telephone directory. 'Yes. I'll be with you in about ten minutes.' She hung up and looked at Lauren.

'I told her she can stay here tonight. I'm sorry, I didn't know what else to say.'

'Of course she can stay. She can share with Cassie, she has twin beds in her room so her friends can sleep over,' Lauren explained to Joe. 'But you should tell Leo we've found her.'

'I promised her I wouldn't tell Leo where she was.'

'You don't have to tell him where she is. Just say we've found her and she's safe.'

⋆   ⋆   ⋆

Alice knew it wasn't going to be an easy conversation. His first words were, 'Where is she?'

'I promised I wouldn't tell you where she is but she's not far away. I'm going to go and get her now. She's scared, Leo. She's afraid the operation will go wrong.'

'And who put that idea in her head, I wonder?'

Alice could hear the anger in his voice and she was glad she wasn't still at the shopping centre. 'I'll try and get her to speak to you, Leo, but for the moment just be glad she's safe.'

She hung up before he could ask any more questions and grabbed her car keys. She dropped a quick kiss on her sister's cheek. 'Thanks, Lauren.'

11

Alice found the place she was looking for, a semi-detached house on a quiet street. Two cars took up most of the short drive and a child's bike was propped against the wall by the front door. She rang the bell, hoping Tiffany hadn't changed her mind.

The door was opened after a couple of minutes by a rather harassed-looking man. He had a mug in one hand and a mobile phone in the other. He motioned Alice to come in and shut the door behind her.

'Sorry, Bob,' he said into the phone. 'Bit of a madhouse at the moment. I'll call you back.' He turned to Alice. 'Sorry we can't put Tiffany up overnight. We just don't have the room.'

He opened a door into a living space dominated by an enormous television screen and an equally massive leather sofa. The sofa was bouncing beneath four boys of varying ages arguing over the remote control. Tiffany was sitting on an upright chair on the other side of the room, a mug in her hand. A girl of about seventeen was sitting on the floor at her feet.

Tiffany stood up when Alice came in, looking relieved. 'Thank you for letting me stay with you, Emily,' she told the girl on the floor. 'Perhaps you can come and visit me in LA one day. I really mean it. We have a big house, so there's plenty of room.'

Tiffany hadn't yet learned the art of diplomacy and Alice hoped that Emily would take the invitation in the generous spirit in which it was meant. The man, whom Alice assumed was the children's father, came back into the room.

'Sorry about the chaos, my wife's at a school meeting, but it's usually like this anyway.' He reached out and snatched the remote control from the boy who was waving it triumphantly at the screen. 'Stop right now, or I'll flush this down the toilet. None of you have any idea how to work the TV without it, so then we might get some peace.'

The four boys looked sullenly at their father. The smallest one folded his arms defiantly.

'*I* know how to change channels without it.'

'Move one inch, Sammy, and you'll go the same way as the TV controller.' He turned to Alice. 'Thank you for coming over. My wife isn't here and I didn't know who to call. Tiffany is welcome to visit any time, as long as she lets her family know where she is.'

Tiffany slowly got to her feet. 'Thank you, Mr Stapleford. I'm sorry to have put you to so much trouble.'

'No trouble at all,' the man answered quickly, but he looked relieved that one of his problems was now sorted.

Alice held out her hand to Tiffany. 'Let's get you home.'

Tiffany didn't want to talk on the drive back, and after ascertaining that she had eaten, Alice didn't push her. Actually, she felt rather cross. *Most people have to face problems in this life,* she thought. *It depends on you how you deal with them.*

Lauren met them at the door. 'I'm really sorry. Leo's here.'

Tiffany looked at Alice accusingly. 'You told him!'

'No, I didn't. Neither did Lauren. I expect he managed to work it out all by himself.' Still feeling cross and not wanting to face Leo when he was in a mood, she thought of going straight up to bed and leaving them to get on with it. Instead she took Tiffany's hand and practically dragged the girl into the kitchen.

'Don't ever do anything like that again,' Leo said with such venom in his voice Tiffany backed away. 'I dropped your mother off at the house. She's having a nervous breakdown.'

'She has them all the time,' Tiffany said sullenly. 'I won't go back with you. Not if my mom's there. She's probably got a posse of doctors round her bed by now.'

It was like a contest, Alice thought, to see who could get the most attention for the longest time. Tiffany had been winning, but now Caroline was fighting back, and Leo was piggy in the middle yet again.

'I thought you'd need your own space tonight, Tiffany, so I've given you my bed,' Lauren said cheerfully. 'I did change the sheets. I'll sleep with Cassie.'

'You don't have to do that.' All the bravado had gone and Tiffany looked as if she was about to burst into tears. 'I've messed up and I'm real sorry.'

'So come back with me,' Leo said. 'Mother's resting. She won't be putting in an appearance for a while.'

'No.' Lauren put her arm round Tiffany. 'Let her stay here tonight. She needs time to sort things out in her head.'

Joe had kept quiet, but now he got to his feet. 'Let the girls look after her, mate. It's probably best if we get out of their hair and let them all get some sleep.' He walked towards the door. 'The girls don't need us here any longer, so we might as well both go home.'

Lauren stood on tiptoe to give Joe a quick kiss. 'Thanks, baby, you've been brilliant. Give me a ring tomorrow.'

Once the men had left, Alice went upstairs with Tiffany to show her where she would be sleeping.

'You've both been so kind, and I know I'm being stupid, but Dr Grant and my mom keep telling me different things,' the girl murmured. 'I really thought I wanted the operation, but now I'm just not sure any more.'

'Don't worry about it tonight. We'll weigh up all the pros and cons in the morning and you can decide what's best. You don't have to do this on your own, Tiffany. We'll all help you.'

They had been talking softly, but Alice heard Cassie grumble and went into her bedroom.

'Who's here?' the little girl asked sleepily.

'Tiffany. She's having a sleepover.'

'Good. I like her. She's got pretty hair, like a princess.'

Alice kissed her niece goodnight and went downstairs, wondering why Cassie had such an obsession with hair.

Lauren had made hot chocolate and handed Alice a mug. She'd whipped the chocolate to a froth and little marshmallows floated on top. 'I thought we both needed something warm and comforting,' she explained. 'How is she?'

'Tired, I think, and very confused. I blame Caroline for this. Tiffany was quite happy to have the operation before her mother arrived on the scene. Now she hasn't a clue what to do for the best. Everyone's telling her something different.'

Lauren waited until Alice sat down next to her. 'Caroline is Tiffany's mother, and I can understand how she feels. Leo decided it would be a good idea if the operation was done by his father, and then went ahead and organised it all without consulting her. I'm sure Tiffany needs the operation if she wants to get her sight back, but Caroline has read all about it online and frightened herself to death. Now she's trying to talk Tiffany out of it.' Lauren took a sip of her drink. 'I'd do the same.'

'Why on earth would you do that?'

'Because if it was Cassie, I'd be scared to death.'

Neither of them wanted to talk any more, so they put the mugs in the dishwasher, turned out the lights, and went upstairs to bed. Alice was sure that the situation would seem clearer in the morning. It usually did.

★　★　★

Leo had parked his car on the street next to Joe's and both sets of lights flashed simultaneously as they used their key fobs.

'Nice girls, the sisters,' Joe said conversationally, opening the door to his car.

'Yes, they are. Very nice.' Now he knew Tiffany was safe, Leo felt drained. He'd left every shred of emotion at the shopping mall.

'You like Alice, don't you?'

That made him smile. 'And you made it quite clear how you feel about Lauren. Yes, I like Alice a lot, but at the moment I don't know what to do about her.'

'Why's that?'

'I have to go back to America and Alice won't come with me. I asked her to.'

'She's got a life here, and Lauren reckons she loves her teaching job. Besides, she wouldn't want to leave her sister and little Cassie.'

'So what do I do? If Tiff doesn't have the operation, she's going to need me to look after her.'

'Not your job, mate. She's a big girl now.'

Leo could feel resentment bubbling

227

up inside him. What did this stranger know? 'Alice isn't prepared to leave her sister, so why do you expect me to give up on mine?'

Joe just shrugged. 'Suit yourself. It's your choice.'

Yes, it was. His choice. He climbed into his car. Talking to Joe wasn't going to solve his problems. He raised his hand in a perfunctory goodbye and started the engine. All he wanted to do was get home and go to bed.

He drove home quickly along the almost empty streets and made his way quietly into the house. His father's car was parked outside but there was no sign of him in the house. He must have gone to bed, Leo decided. His mother was nowhere to be seen, either, but Grace waylaid him before he could creep upstairs.

'You find her, then?'

'Yes, Alice found her. Tiff took a taxi to see some girl she met on Facebook. She's staying with Alice and Lauren tonight.'

Grace scowled at him. 'You let that girl go, you be sorry. I made coffee.'

He blinked at her. 'What girl?'

All he got was another scowl. 'You know who I mean.'

He shook his head, trying to work out what she was talking about. He was feeling so tired, he couldn't think straight. Perhaps coffee would help. He followed Grace into the kitchen and took the mug she handed him. He expected her to leave him alone and go to bed herself, but she lowered herself into a chair and glared at him across the table.

He rubbed his eyes. 'What?'

'Is the girl having the operation?'

He wished Grace wouldn't call Tiffany 'the girl'.

'I don't know. When it comes down to it, it's her choice. My mother is right. There are alternatives to an operation.'

'No!' Grace shook her head emphatically. 'Dr Grant says she needs the operation and he always knows what is best.'

Leo sighed. Everyone seemed to think they knew what was best for Tiffany. He was the one who had talked her into letting his father operate, and now he was having second thoughts as well. No wonder Tiff was scared. She must feel she was being bulldozed from all sides.

He finished his coffee and Grace leaned forward to refill his mug. 'You have to talk to Alice.'

'I don't know what to say to her, Grace.'

'Then you must decide.' Grace climbed to her feet and walked to the door. 'You're not a child minder.'

Leo sighed as he put his mug in the dishwasher. If the darned woman would talk English instead of gobblede-gook, he might be able to understand her. He still hadn't a clue what she was talking about. He followed Grace into the hall, hoping his mother wasn't lying in wait somewhere, but he made it to his room without seeing anyone and dropped on to his bed with a sigh of relief, glad the day was over.

* * *

The next morning, Alice let Tiffany sleep in. She didn't feel there was any hurry to take her back to Dr Grant's house. Everyone had been so stressed-out the day before, Leo and his mother were probably having a lie-in as well. She smiled to herself. Dr Grant had gone to work yesterday and come home again without having any idea there had been a major crisis.

Lauren had dealt with her first client of the day before Tiffany surfaced. Cassie had been awake for some time, and it had been difficult stopping the child rushing upstairs.

'You know how long Sleeping Beauty stayed asleep,' Lauren told her daughter. 'You just have to be patient.'

Cassie's eyes opened wide with disbelief. 'You mean I have to wait for the prince to come and wake her?'

Alice laughed. 'Maybe not. I think I can hear Tiffany moving around. Why don't you go up and show her where the bathroom is and give her a clean towel from the airing cupboard?'

Cassie disappeared with a little squeak of delight just as Leo's car drew up outside. Alice looked out and sighed.

'He's like the proverbial bad penny. It would have been nice if we could have talked to Tiffany without him around.'

'She is his sister.' Lauren reached for the kettle. 'I've got nearly an hour before my next client. I'll make tea.'

'I had to come over,' Leo said as Alice opened the door. 'I'm not going to get any work done until all this is sorted, and I'm getting near my deadline.' He walked in. 'Where's Tiff?'

Alice led the way into the kitchen. 'She's only just woken up. She'll be down in a minute.' He looked tired, she thought, but she probably looked even worse. She was freshly showered, but with no make-up on and her hair still damp and tied in a ponytail. She was glad she'd changed out of her pyjamas, though. Leo had seen enough of them.

Cassie bounced into the kitchen, coming to a stop when she saw Leo. 'Did you come to wake the princess? She's having a shower, then she said she'll be right down.'

'So I was too late?' Leo said, feigning disappointment. 'The princess woke up all on her own.'

Cassie nodded solemnly. 'You should have come on your horse. That would've been quicker.'

Lauren shook her head in exasperation. 'Get yourself some cereal, Cassie, and perhaps you'll be quiet for five minutes. You can't talk if you're eating.'

Cassie looked surprised. 'Yes, I can.'

Lauren picked Cassie up and plonked her down on a chair at the table. 'Well, don't. It's rude.' She tipped cereal into a bowl, poured on milk, and set it in front of Cassie, handing her a spoon. 'Not another word until that's all gone.' She turned to Leo. 'Sorry about that. I suggest we wait for Tiffany to come downstairs so we don't discuss anything behind her back, and then see if we can sort something out between us.'

'Get your laptop,' Alice suggested. 'I know everyone should take Internet info with a large pinch of salt, but Tiffany will take more notice of what comes up on the screen than anything any of us say to her.'

Lauren nodded. 'If we Google her eye problem, we should get some treatment options.'

Tiffany walked into the room and Alice thought how easily she wore her beauty. She had borrowed a lilac robe that belonged to Lauren and because of her height the robe only just covered her knees, showing long, tanned legs ending in elegant feet. Her bright hair tumbled round her shoulders, freshly washed and gleaming with good health, even though she probably hadn't had a very good night. Alice sighed — at barely twenty-five, she was feeling positively ancient.

'Sit down, Tiffany,' Lauren said. 'What cereal would you like? We have wheat flakes with red berries, some chocolate flavoured thingies, or rice crispies.'

'I don't think I want . . . '

'You have to eat,' Lauren said firmly. 'You should know that. Have the wheat flakes. They taste okay.'

'I'd do what she says,' Alice said. 'Or she'll force-feed you.'

Cassie waved her spoon in the air, showering the table with milk. 'Mummy makes me eat *all* my breakfast.'

Lauren picked up a cloth. 'I said no talking until you finish.' She wiped the table and spooned up the last mouthful of cereal, popping it into Cassie's open mouth. She helped the little girl down from the table and sent her out into the sunny strip of garden. 'Go outside and kill a few dragons, Mummy has work to do.' She fetched her laptop so that they could scan the NHS page on diseases related to diabetes, and Alice re-boiled the kettle and made tea for them all.

'It looks as if surgery is recommended for advanced retinopathy,' Leo said. 'It's usually too late for laser treatment to work. But, look, the operation is done under local anaesthetic and you can go home the next day.'

'So I won't be in hospital for ages?' Tiffany had put on her glasses and was peering at the screen. 'Why did my mother say the operation was dangerous and I might go completely blind?'

'Because she loves you and she's more scared than you are,' Alice said. 'There are risks with any operation, but Dr Grant is the best there is. He won't let anything go wrong.'

'Today's Friday, isn't it? So I just have to get through the weekend and then get it done so we can all go home.'

Leo walked round the table to give his sister a hug. 'I still have my editing to finish, Tiff. I may not be able to come back with you.'

Alice held her breath while Tiffany used her perfect white teeth to chew her bottom lip.

'How long will you be? We can wait a few days — until you finish your editing.'

He dropped a kiss on the bright hair and moved away. 'I'll finish as quickly as I can. Don't worry about it now. Get yourself dressed and I'll take you home.'

So he was taking the easy way out. Alice looked at him as Tiffany left the room, but he avoided her eyes.

'I can work tomorrow, if you like,' she told him. 'I know you want to get the editing finished as soon as possible.'

If he heard the sarcasm in her voice, he ignored it.

'It's Saturday tomorrow.'

She returned his impassive look with one of her own. 'I know, and you don't usually work at the weekend, but if you want to get your book finished in time to go back to America with Tiffany, we need to get a move on.'

He nodded. 'Thank you. I'll see you tomorrow, then, at the usual time. Tell Tiff I'll be waiting in the car.'

He thanked Lauren rather formally for her help and hospitality and walked out of the door.

Alice didn't speak for a moment, because she knew she might cry. She had hoped Leo would still consider staying behind — he had said he wanted to get to know her better — but that idea had obviously gone out of the window. Tiffany was scared and needed him, and that was all he could think about.

One day he might wake up and find that life had gone on without him — but he would do that in America, not in England.

'He had to choose between me and his sister — and Tiffany came first,' she whispered.

'And you let her,' Lauren returned. 'For goodness' sake, Alice, I thought you were a fighter. The poor man is being torn in half. He loves his sister and staying here with you feels like a big betrayal. Men are no good at multi-tasking. They can't think about more than one major thing at a time.'

'So what do I do?'

'Fight back. Give him all the help he

needs to finish the book. That gets one problem out of the way. Be supportive when his sister goes in to hospital, and keep his mother out of his hair.' Lauren smiled. 'In other words, make yourself indispensable.'

When Alice didn't answer, Lauren gave her a hug. 'Only you know whether he's worth it.'

'Oh, he's worth it.' Alice managed a tentative smile. 'But those are two formidable women. If I'm going to take them on, I'll need all the help I can get.'

'Done!' Lauren gave her sister a high-five. 'Joe is already on your side, and you have me and Cassie as well. Together, we'll be invincible.'

12

Alice drove slowly the next morning. She told herself she was enjoying a drive in the late summer sunshine, but in reality she was feeling quite nervous about working with Leo. She would naturally give him all the support he needed — but she didn't intend trapping him into staying in England.

He had to make up his own mind, and he appeared to have done that already.

The scented stock had given way to chrysanthemums, a great swathe of them on the drive up to the house, and they made her smile. It was surely impossible to be miserable on such a beautiful day.

Grace opened the door with a frown on her face. 'Everyone is in a mood. Good job you leave the little one at home.'

Alice sighed. It looked as if it was going to be worse than she had feared. Perhaps she could cheer everyone up.

'Can I pick some chrysanthemums?' she asked Grace. 'Leo might welcome a touch of colour on his desk.'

She could tell by the expression on Grace's face that her suggestion wasn't expected to produce results, but by the time she had gathered a small bunch, Grace had produced a pretty jug from the kitchen. She carried her offering to the library, determined to remain cheerful whatever sort of mood Leo might be in. As it was, he greeted her with a smile.

'Are those for me?'

She handed him the jug. 'To cheer you up on a sunny day.'

'Thank you, Alice.' He moved some papers so he could stand the flowers on the desk. 'I have to apologise for the way I behaved last night. Tiffany is scared, so there was a reason for her lack of gratitude, but I have no excuse. You and Lauren were brilliant. Not only did you find Tiff and bring her home, but you gave her a room for the night and space to think things through. I can't thank you enough.'

She hated it when he went all formal on her and used words instead of emotion. He did that a lot — putting a barrier of words between them so he wouldn't show his true feelings.

She shrugged. 'We would have done the same for anyone.'

For a moment he looked confused. 'Right. Just so you know that I'm really grateful.'

She gave him a cool smile. 'Yes. You said that already. It was really nothing.'

He sorted out the work they still needed to get through and handed her a sheaf of paper. 'I marked the obvious edits on the hard copy.'

He was obviously not sure how to behave, and she wasn't going to help him out. He couldn't make her a daisy chain and kiss her passionately one day, treat her like a paid employee the next, and expect her to switch roles as it suited him. If formality was what he wanted, that was what he would get.

She spent the next two hours working through the hard copy, editing on the screen, and checking with Leo whenever the edits didn't agree. This was the end of the book and Lyra was about to win the day.

For some reason, she felt sorry for the villain. He was a nasty piece of work, but he hadn't actually killed anyone. She looked up at Leo who was pacing the room.

'Does Lyra kill the villain in the end?'

He stopped pacing and looked at her in surprise. 'Of course.'

'He made a mistake, but that doesn't mean he should die.'

'You haven't finished the book yet, and you're not a writer. How would you know what I should do with my villain? The villain always gets killed in the end.'

'But I am a reader, and I don't want him killed. He's already been punished enough. He didn't know what path to take and he took the wrong one. We all make mistakes but we don't deserve to die for them. Lyra wouldn't kill him — it's out of character.'

He frowned at her. 'She just did.'

'Then that makes her the villain, not him. She'll regret her decision and have to live with it for the rest of her life.'

'This is fiction, Alice, not real life. The villain getting killed at the end is traditional.'

She smiled at him. 'Do you really want to be 'traditional', Leo? You might find it fun to rock the boat a little and do something mad for a change.'

'Thanks for the suggestion, and I agree I need to be different. That's why I've got a feisty protagonist. When you read the end of the book you'll realise I'm definitely not traditional.'

Before she had time to back away, he caught hold of her and gave her a resounding kiss. 'See? I'm always innovative, unpredictable. Nothing traditional about me.'

She tried to disregard the kiss. He

was making a point, nothing more, but there was an odd look in his eye that made her back away nervously. 'I was thinking maybe Lyra could ditch the hero and marry the villain, but perhaps that's going too far.'

'There is no way she would marry the villain. She's far too independent. Besides, I need her to be free of romantic entanglements for another book. You can stop fretting. She won't kill him, he'll shoot himself in the end. His guilt proves too much for him.'

He caught Alice's hands again and pulled her towards him. 'I've had time to think things through. I'll have to go back to America with Tiff and my mother because that's what I promised, but I'll come back as soon as I can. I don't want to lose you, Alice.'

She told herself she had to be content with that. She wasn't going to spoil the few days they had left together, but she was under no illusion that he would really give up everything for her. He might genuinely believe he would, but once he got back to America and resumed his old life, she would become nothing more than a pleasant memory.

So be it, she thought philosophically. She would make sure that she was the best memory he'd ever had.

'If we finish this lot of work today, can we go out somewhere tomorrow?' she asked. 'Maybe that pub by the river again.'

He dropped a kiss on the tip of her nose. 'That's a great idea. Tiff will need something to take her mind off the operation. We'll take her to the inn and have lunch there. She'll love that.'

Alice stared at him. That wasn't what she meant at all.

'You did mean for Tiff to come with us, didn't you? It will help her relax. She's like a wound spring at the moment.'

'Of course,' Alice answered brightly. 'That was my plan.' She was trying very hard to follow Lauren's advice and be supportive. 'I can stay a bit later today because I don't have Cassie, so all I need to do on Monday is read everything through for the last time.'

'I'll be at the hospital most of the day.'

'I know, but Lauren only has a couple of half-hour appointments. If she can keep Cassie at home with her, it won't be a problem.'

'You're an angel.' He kissed her again, and this time he took his time about it.

'I so wish I didn't have to go back to America, but Tiff will have to be careful on the flight. My dad is using silicone oil in her eye so there's no restriction on her flying, but she'll still need someone to take care of her — you know what my mother's like.'

Pretty useless, Alice thought. But the woman did her best. It wasn't Caroline's fault Tiffany had never been allowed to grow up. If it weren't for her over-protective brother, she would have been allowed to make the usual mistakes that were part of becoming an adult. Most young people coped with diabetes exceedingly well.

★ ★ ★

Alice wasn't sure how she managed to get through the rest of the day. Lunch was a strained affair with Caroline behaving with a forced brightness that fooled no one, and Tiffany sullen and mostly silent. Leo tried to keep a conversation of some sort going, but eventually gave up, and Alice wished with all her heart she hadn't offered to stay.

The whole thing was ridiculous. The operation might be tricky but it was relatively minor as operations went, and all the melodrama associated with it was beginning to get her down.

'That was fun, wasn't it?' Leo said as they walked back to the library. 'My sister is becoming as much of a drama queen as my mother. I just want Monday over so we can get back to normal. I had a word with my father.

They may keep Tiff in overnight. He still has some tests to do before he operates so the hospital stay may run on into Tuesday.'

'Will you stay at the hospital overnight as well?'

He gave her a rueful smile. 'You think that I'm overreacting, don't you?'

'A little. Tiffany's mother will be with her.' When he didn't say anything, she sighed. 'I know you think Caroline is useless, but perhaps that's because you've always looked after Tiffany. If you hadn't been around, she'd have managed without you.'

He frowned. 'I tried that, didn't I? The only time Tiff went away on her own, she finished up in hospital.'

'But she realised she'd been stupid, and dealt with it. She explained what had happened to her agency and went home to America — to her mother. Caroline might not be so useless if she didn't have you to rely on all the time. She might actually start behaving like a mother.'

Leo was sorting papers that didn't need sorting. 'She lost her half-blind daughter in a shopping mall — that's how good a mother she is.'

Alice thought she might have gone too far, but she couldn't stop now. He was behaving like an idiot. 'That's unfair. It wasn't your mother's fault Tiffany left the shopping centre. She was completely selfish and took off without telling anyone where she was going. But she managed to find her way across town to visit a friend she's never met before. She may have trouble seeing, but she's far from helpless.'

'I think we've done enough work for one day.' Leo turned to her, his face expressionless. 'I think I know my sister better than you. At the moment she's scared and needs my support. I'm not going to abandon her, Alice. Don't ever think that.'

She was surprised that golden eyes could look so cool. 'Does that mean tomorrow's off, then?' she asked rather flippantly. She realised too late that she'd definitely overstepped the mark. That was one of her failings — never knowing when to keep her mouth shut.

'What you do tomorrow is up to you, but we've finished here for today. If your offer still stands and you can come in on Monday to finish up, I would appreciate it.'

He was going all formal on her again.

'I keep my promises, Leo. I'll be here on Monday, and in case I don't see her, please give my best wishes to Tiffany.'

Alice grabbed her bag from the desk and almost ran from the room, fighting back angry tears. How could he change so quickly? One minute he was kissing her and the next minute he was asking her to leave. It was just as well he was going back to America. They were obviously incompatible.

★ ★ ★

After Alice had gone, Leo paced the room trying to work out what had just happened. Whatever it was, he decided, it wasn't his fault. She had no right telling him how to manage his own family. She'd only been around five minutes and she was already telling him how to run his life.

He walked across to a cabinet under the bookshelves. His father's bottle of single malt was still in the same place and this was definitely one of those occasions that called for a strong drink. He was just pouring himself a generous measure when the door opened and the doctor walked into the room.

'Make that two. I've had one hell of a day.'

Leo poured whisky into a second glass. 'Mine hasn't been too great, either. I think I just had a major falling-out with Alice.'

'Pity.' His father sank into the leather chair behind the desk. 'She seems like a nice, sensible girl.'

'Maybe. But add interfering, bossy, and opinionated to that.'

His father managed a rare grin. 'A typical woman, by the sound of it.

You're lucky to have someone to argue with. Grace isn't exactly the master of scintillating rhetoric. Sometimes I wish your mother was still around, just for the arguments we used to have.'

'She misses you, too.'

Peter Grant sat up in his chair. 'Did she actually say that?'

'Several times.' Leo had no desire to talk about his mother. There were more important things he needed to discuss with his father. 'Is this operation really safe, Dad? Tiffany ran away and Mother's freaking out. I know she's always been neurotic, but maybe this time she has cause.'

'I've decided to operate on only one eye. The retinal detachment is confined to the left eye, so that's the one we'll operate on, and a patch over one eye will be easier for Tiffany to handle.' The doctor seemed to realise, belatedly, what Leo had said. 'She ran away? Why?'

'Because she's scared. Mother's been telling her about all the things that can go wrong with the operation. You really need to talk to Tiff.'

The doctor downed the rest of his whisky. 'I need to talk to your mother. She must know I would never do anything to endanger my stepdaughter. Tiffany will get the best treatment I can give her. Once Caroline realises that, perhaps she can explain it in a way the girl can understand. I won't operate on a reluctant patient.'

And that was exactly what he might get. Leo hoped a day out, with lunch at that pretty little pub, would take his sister's mind off Monday. It would be nice if Alice decided to come as well, but he was fast realising he had no idea how her mind worked.

★   ★   ★

At that moment, Alice was telling Lauren exactly how she felt about Leo Grant.

'So you're not going out with him tomorrow?'

'Why would I?' Alice said huffily. 'He's got this appendage called Tiffany who always goes where he goes. I think they're really conjoined twins. You never actually see them apart.'

'Now you're just being silly,' Lauren said dismissively. 'I thought you were going to put up a fight, not fall at the first hurdle. You know he feels responsible for his sister. I feel the same about you.'

Alice looked surprised. 'You do?'

'Of course I do. I worry about getting too attached to Joe because I'd have to leave you on your own. I worry about you working too hard at the school, and I worry about dumping Cassie on you all the time. If you were having an operation that might make you go blind, I'd be climbing the walls.'

Near to tears, Alice gave her sister a hug. 'Please don't give up Joe on my account. I'd never forgive myself.' She stepped back. 'Has he already proposed?'

'Goodness, no!' Lauren laughed.

'That's a long way in the future, but I really like him a lot.' She busied herself filling the kettle. 'I thought you fancied Leo.'

Alice got mugs out of the cupboard, thinking that the two of them worked like a well-oiled team. She'd miss that — but she would never stand in Lauren's way.

'I do fancy him. I fancy him a lot, actually, and I am prepared to fight for him. I'll slay the dragon if I have to. But I can't compete with Tiffany. She has no idea that she's ruining her brother's life.'

'Slay the dragon? Where did that come from?'

Alice shook her head. 'It's not important. So you think I should go along on this trip tomorrow? Play piggy in the middle?'

Lauren dropped tea bags into the mugs and poured juice into a beaker for Cassie. 'Better than piggy on the outside.'

Cassie took the drink her mother

handed her. 'I know This Little Piggy Went To Market. I can sing it, too.'

Alice gave her sister a long speculative look. 'Are you seeing Joe tomorrow?'

'We might take Cassie out. But you can come too.'

'Stop right now. I'm fine on my own. But I was thinking you might like a day out with Joe. Just the two of you. How about I take Cassie with me?'

'To the pub for lunch? With Leo and Tiffany?'

'Then I won't have to play piggy. If Leo can bring his sister, I can bring my niece. She loves being with Leo.' She turned to Cassie. 'You'd like to go out with Leo tomorrow, wouldn't you? We're going to have lunch at a pub and Tiffany's coming with us as well, so you can show her how to feed the ducks on the river.'

Cassie clapped her hands. 'Can we take bread with us?'

Lauren smiled. 'If anyone can take Tiffany's mind off her operation, Cassie can.'

Alice grinned at her sister. 'Just being supportive.' She grabbed the phone and dialled Leo's number. 'What time are you picking me up tomorrow?' The silence on the other end of the line made her want to laugh. 'I'm bringing Cassie with me. I've promised her we'll let her feed the ducks.'

It took him a minute to answer. 'Great,' he said at last. 'I'll pick you up about midday. If we leave it too late, we won't get a table. They don't take bookings.'

'How did he take it?' Lauren asked.

'It takes a lot to disconcert Leo. You'd have thought we parted on the best of terms. At least he'll have to behave himself in front of Cassie.'

'I'm going to have lunch with the prince and the princess,' Cassie said happily.

'Yeah,' Alice said darkly. 'There's nothing quite like lunch with the royal family.'

★ ★ ★

Sunday morning started off cloudy, but by mid-morning the sun was out and the birds were singing. Alice dressed carefully. It was impossible to compete with a tall, redheaded model, but she had every intention of doing her best. She decided to go casual. The day was going to be warm enough for her denim shorts and she knew they made her legs look longer.

She needed every advantage she could get. Leo was used to beauty. He lived in LA where even the pensioners were gorgeous — and he had grown up with Tiffany.

The top Alice chose was pale lemon, sleeveless, and clung in all the right places. Not wanting to overdo it, she slipped her feet into flip-flops, but not until she had painted her toenails fuchsia pink.

Cassie insisted on wearing a dress and having a bow in her hair. Lauren said it didn't matter if she got dirty. 'Just don't let her fall in the river.'

Leo arrived on time, looking every

inch the prince. His jeans were snug, his shirt showed off his broad chest, and the sun highlighted his hair with copper streaks. He looked like a clothed version of Michelangelo's David. Tiffany stayed in the back of the car, enormous sunglasses covering most of her face.

Alice slipped Cassie's booster seat in the back of the car next to Tiffany. 'She's not allowed in the front because of the airbag,' she informed nobody in particular. That just meant she had to sit in the front next to Leo. Not too much of a hardship, she decided, as she fastened her seat belt.

Leo parked the car outside the Swan and grabbed a table half in and half out of the shade. Alice sat in the sun, revelling in the warmth on her bare arms, but she made sure Cassie was in the shade.

Tiffany stayed in the car to use her insulin pen but once they were seated she perked up, pointing out some baby ducklings that were following their mother into the water. 'Can they swim from the time they're born?' she mused. 'I suppose they must, otherwise they'd drown.'

'Ducks can't drown,' Cassie informed her. 'Ducks float.'

'Everyone knows that,' Leo added. 'Even those yellow plastic ones float. You should know that, Tiffany.'

Alice remembered they hadn't tried the food when they were here last, which made her think of daisy chains and other things. She ordered roast chicken for herself and a child's portion for Cassie, while Leo went with the roast beef and Tiffany decided to try spring lamb with mint sauce.

'I've never had mint sauce before,' she said happily. 'Or Jersey Royals. I don't know what those are.'

By the time Tiffany had got through half a pint of ale and eaten every scrap of her meal, she seemed much more relaxed. They left the pub to walk along the riverbank and Alice wondered if Leo was having the same sense of déjà vu. She could almost feel his mouth on hers, and slipped a sideways glance at him to find him looking back at her. He smiled, and she felt her stomach flip in response. Lauren was right. She couldn't let this man go without a fight.

Tiffany clung to Leo's arm, worried about being so close to the bank, so once Cassie had fed the ducks they stopped for a rest and Tiffany sat beside Alice on the soft grass. Leo wandered off and they let him go, chatting about make-up and clothes until he came back and told them it was time to leave.

It had been a successful afternoon, Alice decided, as she slipped into her seat beside him. Tiffany seemed much more relaxed and Leo was no longer in a foul mood. Cassie fell asleep on the way home, and Leo carried her into the house without waking her.

'Put her on the sofa,' Lauren said with a smile of thanks. 'She'll wake up in her own time. Why don't you get Tiffany out of the car and you can both come in for a cup of tea?'

13

Alice knew Lauren was desperate to meet the infamous Tiffany, and Leo couldn't very well turn down her invitation without appearing rude. He only hesitated a moment, and then thanked Lauren and went to tell Tiffany they were stopping for tea. They left the sleeping Cassie on the sofa and sat round the kitchen table. Tiffany made all the right noises about how nice the house was and then asked Lauren about her hairdressing business.

'I wish I could have my hair done before I go into hospital,' Tiffany remarked. 'I've let it get far too long.'

'I can give you a quick tidy-up right now, if you like,' Lauren offered. 'It won't take more than half an hour and Alice can watch Cassie if she wakes.' She picked up a strand of Tiffany's hair and let it run through her fingers.

'When Alice described your hair, I was sure that you would have had it coloured professionally, but it's natural, isn't it? You are so lucky. I'd make an absolute fortune if I could duplicate that particular shade of red.'

'Sometimes I'd like to change it and try something different, but it's my signature colour now. The agency insists I keep it exactly that shade.'

While Lauren worked on Tiffany's hair, Alice took Leo outside to look at their little garden. She could see Cassie through the French doors, in case the little girl woke up suddenly.

Once they were alone, Leo took her hand in his. 'Thank you.'

'What for?' She could feel her face going pink and wondered why she was suddenly behaving like a schoolgirl. 'I pretty well gatecrashed the party. I know you didn't really want me along, so I invited myself.'

'Maybe. But look at the difference it made to Tiffany. You're amazing, Alice. You have this wonderful knack of cheering people up.'

'Don't I just,' she agreed. Little Miss Sunshine, that's who she was. Always on hand to cheer people up. But could he, just once, not talk about his sister? she wondered.

Probably not. Besides, she quite liked Tiffany. Although she'd like her even more if the redhead was safely on the other side of the ocean.

'Tiffany will be fine,' she told Leo. He was still holding her hand and she tried to pull it away, but he hung on to it so she left it where it was. 'I feel sorry for your mother, all alone at the house. We should have taken her with us.'

He laughed, swapping the hand-holding for an arm round her shoulders. 'The idea was to calm Tiff down, remember? My mother makes her anxious and worried even when there's nothing to worry about.'

'It's not easy being a single parent, Leo. Lauren knows all about that. Your mother not only had you to look after, she had a new baby and no husband or partner to help her. Also, she was in a strange country.'

'That was her decision.' His shoulders lifted in a sigh. 'I've tried to help her. Believe me, I've tried. But she turns every minor problem into a crisis and it gets very tiring after a while. She's had guys who've been interested in her, but every time she drives them away, always worrying obsessively about one thing or another. At least my father was able to ride the storm and let her get on with it. He just used to take himself off to work, out of the way.'

'Why did she leave him, Leo?'

'Another man. An American businessman in England for a conference. When he asked her to go to America with him, he thought she was going to leave me with my father; that was his first shock. Then she got pregnant. He only lasted about a month after that.'

'Why didn't she come back to England?'

'To what? She didn't think my father would take her back, not after what she'd done — and she knew that Grace would never forgive her.'

'So how long has she been divorced?' Alice asked.

'From my father?' He looked surprised. 'She isn't. She never asked for a divorce and he wouldn't have given her one if she had. I think he still loves her.'

Alice was shocked into silence. So Dr Grant was still married to Caroline. That's why Tiffany still had the same surname.

'Would he have her back, do you think?'

Leo shrugged. 'Probably. But he'd never give her the attention she needs. He's too self-centred, and so is she.'

Leo bent to pick a pansy, and tucked it into Alice's hair. 'Every time she had one of her turns, he'd go off to work and leave her to it, and that's not what she wants.'

Alice touched the flower in her hair and smiled up at him. 'You have quite a romantic streak at times.'

'I do, don't I?'

He still had his arm round her shoulders and it took him barely a second to pull her against him. She could feel his heart beating strongly through the thin cotton of his shirt. She tried to move away, but as his arms tightened round her and his mouth came down on hers, the thought of moving anywhere else went straight out of her head as she was completely enveloped by a wave of pleasure.

The kiss could have gone on forever if she hadn't seen Cassie sit up on the sofa, from the corner of her eye.

She freed herself from Leo's arms with a little moan of frustration. 'Cassie's awake! I don't know whether she saw us.'

But when she pushed open the French door, Alice was pleased to see that Cassie was still half asleep.

'Wake up, sweetheart, or you'll fall off the sofa,' she told her niece affection-ately. 'Mummy's styling Tiffany's hair, do you want to go and see?'

Leo picked the little girl up and sat

her on his hip. Alice wished he'd pick her up as well. Her legs were feeling decidedly wobbly. Her brain told her that she shouldn't let him kiss her whenever he felt like it — but when it actually happened her body told her something completely different.

Still feeling confused and unsure what to do, she followed Leo and Cassie into the conservatory where Lauren was blow-drying Tiffany's hair.

'She's amazing, your sister.' Tiffany peered at herself in the mirror. 'As long as I get close enough, I can still see pretty good. I pay my stylist over a hundred dollars and I never look this cool.'

Lauren laughed. 'Well, I'm obviously undercharging my clients — but they don't have hair like yours. I'll happily do yours for free any day.'

Tiffany stood up and Lauren helped her out of the gown. 'Now it's time for that tea I promised you.' She took the still-sleepy Cassie from Leo and sat her at the table. 'Do you want some milk and a piece of cake?'

Cassie looked shyly at Leo. 'Is the prince having cake?'

He laughed and sat next to her. 'You betcha, princess. All princes love cake.'

'How come you're a prince?' Tiffany asked.

'It's a title I deserve, don't you think?' He ignored her look of amused derision. 'It just took Princess Cassie here to realise my true worth.'

Lauren fetched the chocolate cake from the fridge and brought mugs of tea to the table.

Tiffany looked delighted. 'We don't have afternoon tea, do we, Leo? It's not something we do in America. We must be sure to take some tea back with us. It will be better for us than all that coffee, I think.'

Alice had almost forgotten — it was only a few days before Leo would be leaving. She saw Lauren looking at her and forced a smile. 'I'll get you some teabags to take back with you,' she said brightly. 'That's not a problem. Let me know if there's anything else you want.'

Tiffany shook her head. 'You know, I just want to get this whole thing over with and go home. Dr Grant is only operating on one of my eyes and, depending on the MRI, I may not need to have the other one done at all. He says that either way, I shall be able to see a lot better than I can now.'

Alice gave Tiffany a hug before she left and wished her luck. 'Not that you need good luck so much as a good surgeon, and you've got that,' she added reassuringly.

She promised Leo she would be at the house in the morning. 'I'll finish checking continuity, like page numbers and chapter headings, and leave it ready for you. Give me a ring to let me know when Tiffany goes in to surgery.'

She walked with them to the car and for a moment Leo looked as if he was about to say something, but then he turned to help his sister into the front seat and drove away without looking back.

★ ★ ★

'You will see him again, won't you?' Lauren asked when Alice trailed disconsolately back into the house.

'I don't know.'

Alice felt a great sadness settle over her. What if she didn't see Leo again? Would he go back to Los Angeles and forget all about her — or would he realise how much he missed her and get the next plane back to England? They were questions she couldn't answer. She had refused to go with him, refused to give up her life in England for him, and she was beginning to wonder whether she had made a mistake.

No — she *had* done the right thing. It was just too soon in their relationship for her to make a life-changing decision like that. She really didn't know Leo Grant well enough yet.

'How about you and Joe?' she asked, trying to change the subject. 'How are things going with you two?'

Lauren smiled. 'I really like him and

he makes a real fuss of Cassie, but . . . '

'But what? He's got a wife hidden away somewhere?'

'Goodness, no. Nothing like that. It was something he said. It was a bit of a shock really, because I hadn't thought about it and I should have done.'

'Lauren, you're driving me mad. What did he say?'

'He just happened to mention in passing that he wants children of his own.'

'Children!' Alice raised her hands in mock horror. 'How many, exactly?'

Lauren blushed. 'Probably one would do, but I can't have a baby, can I? It would be ridiculous.'

'Why is it ridiculous? There's nothing wrong with you, is there? Did something happen when you had Cassie, something you didn't tell me about?'

Lauren shook her head. 'Of course not. I'm absolutely fine. But I'm thirty-one in a couple of months. I can't have another baby. I'm too old.'

'No, you're right.' Alice sat down

next to her sister on the sofa. 'You might be an old lady of, oooh, almost forty by the time your child started school. Just imagine being on the school run with white hair and all those wrinkles.'

'Oh, stop it, Alice,' Lauren said impatiently. 'I have Cassie to think about, as well. She's still my baby.'

'She'd be ecstatic. She's always wanted a sister.'

Lauren blinked back tears and smiled. 'I can't promise her that.' She wiped a hand across her eyes. 'I've been worrying about it for days. You really think it would be okay? It would mean starting all over again.'

'Exactly. Go for it, Lauren. You're a wonderful mother — and your little princess would love to have a baby brother or sister.'

Lauren took a deep breath. 'You really think I can do it?'

'I know you can.'

Lauren laughed. 'I'm getting way ahead of myself here, you know. I need to get to know Joe a lot better before I commit to a life of nappies and sleepless nights. I've done it once and I know how awful it is at times.'

Alice was silent. She was pleased her sister's love life was working out so well. If anyone deserved a little happiness, Lauren did. But Leo was flying back to America, and there was no hope of a wedding or babies coming her way.

'You could go with him, you know,' Lauren said softly, 'back to America. I'm not on my own any more.'

Alice shook her head. 'No. If he stays any longer I shall fall in love with him, I know that, but I'm not prepared to share him. I need him to put me first for once.'

'Hmmm, I can see that might be tricky. Goodness, you've got his mother to contend with as well, haven't you? Joe hasn't got any family now his dad is gone. I think that's why he's so desperate to have a family of his own.'

Alice gave her sister a hug. 'Give him what he wants, then. Just remind him I count as family as well. Be happy, Lauren.'

Alice slept surprisingly well, considering, waking as the sunlight shafted through her blinds.

The day of the operation. She looked at her watch. Tiffany and her mother would be leaving soon. Leo was driving them to the hospital and Doctor Grant would meet them there. He had spent the night at the hospital so he could clear his workload and give Tiffany his undivided attention for the day.

Although the operation itself wouldn't take very long, there were scans to be done beforehand and careful monitoring procedures afterwards. He also had a very nervous patient and a neurotic mother who would need careful handling.

Leo didn't need to be there at all. He would just get in everyone's way.

When she walked into the kitchen, Alice knew at once that something was wrong. Cassie was already dressed, with ribbons in her hair, and Lauren was looking guilty.

'Is there any chance,' she asked, as she poured tea for Alice, 'that you could take Cassie with you this morning? You know that woman who came in for a cut and finish? The one I told you has a yacht in the Bahamas? Well, she's getting married in a couple of weeks and she just phoned to ask if I can fit her in for a colouring job today — like, six separate highlights — and she says if she likes what I do, she'll send all her bridesmaids to me to have their hair done before the wedding.'

Lauren stopped to draw a breath. 'I really need the work, Alice — and I can't risk ruining the woman's hair because I have to watch Cassie. She's promised me she won't get under anyone's feet.'

Alice had intended driving over and getting the work finished as quickly as she could, but Lauren was right. A recommendation like that could mean another sink in the conservatory and maybe an assistant.

Cassie jumped down from her chair and came to stand by Alice. 'I won't be under feet. I'll bake cakes with Grace.'

Alice hugged her niece. 'You're never any bother, sweetheart. Don't worry about it, Lauren. I'll have the house to myself apart from Grace. So there won't be any feet for Cassie to get under.'

Lauren smiled with relief. 'I've done nothing but ask for favours recently. I feel really guilty. But there is some good news. Joe says the new boiler has arrived and he can put it in next week. He's only charging us what he had to pay for it and nothing for installation, so we're getting it pretty cheap. It's not going to take all your money.'

'It's not 'my' money, it's boiler money,' Alice said firmly. 'Anything left over belongs to both of us. We'll go out on the town to celebrate once the new boiler is up and running. I might even treat Joe, too, to thank him.'

By the time the boiler was in, Leo would have left for America, and she'd need a posh meal out somewhere to cheer her up.

No doubt she would get over him eventually, she decided philosophically, but it was going to hurt for a long time.

He really was the man of her dreams — and perhaps one day, if Tiffany eventually managed to grow up and take care of herself, Leo would come back to England for a visit.

Not that she was going to wait for him, or anything — but she hadn't met anyone she wanted to spend the rest of her life with yet, so he might still be in with a chance.

She smiled to herself. She was still living in a dream world.

★ ★ ★

The house was quiet when she parked outside. There were no cars in the driveway and no Grace at the door to meet them — and Alice was sure Leo must have mentioned she would be coming over to work. She helped Cassie out, reprimanding her for having unfastened her seat belt while they were still moving.

'Where's Grace?' Cassie asked, as Alice knocked on the front door.

'She's probably outside in the garden and didn't hear us drive up. She'll answer the door in a minute.'

'It's open,' Cassie said, pushing the heavy door wide. 'Can we go in and find her?'

Alice stepped inside the hallway, thinking Grace had probably unlatched the door before she went outside, but it was still odd to find it open. Cassie bounded down the hall towards the kitchen with Alice hot on her heels. 'Wait for me, Cassie.'

But Grace wasn't in the kitchen. Puzzled, Alice looked outside. Grace could be anywhere. Catching hold of Cassie's hand, she headed for the library. If Grace had gone out somewhere, there might be a problem. She wasn't sure whether she could keep an eye on Cassie and do her editing.

The first thing she noticed was a

sheet of paper propped up on the desk.

I am in my room. I make lunch for you later.

Alice looked at Cassie. The little girl was staring at her wide-eyed. 'Is that a letter from Grace?'

Alice nodded. 'Maybe she's not feeling very well. She says she's in her room, so we'd better go and find her and see if she needs anything.'

'I know where her room is. She's got a little garden of her own. I'd like a garden all my own. I could grow nice things, like strawberries.'

Cassie led the way into the garden and round the side of the house. A small, hidden courtyard was filled with pots. The geraniums were finished, but pansies tumbled from tubs and brilliantly coloured petunias filled hanging baskets. French doors were open, sheer curtains fluttering in the breeze.

Grace must have heard them coming because she called from inside. 'Come in, Alice.' She was sitting on an upright wooden chair beside a small table. 'It's the bones in the back of me,' she said, reaching behind her. 'Sometimes they seize up and I have to sit on a hard chair.'

'You've put your back out? Oh, you poor thing. Don't move,' Alice said hurriedly as Grace was about to stand up. 'Do you need a doctor?'

The woman shook her head, wincing as she did so. 'No. I have pills.' She pointed to a small bottle on the table.

'But you don't have any water to swallow them with.'

Alice looked around and saw they were in what was really a small apartment. An open door led to a tiny kitchen, and a closed door on the other side of the room probably opened into a bedroom. She walked into the spotless little kitchen and found a glass on the work surface. She filled it with water and set it on the table next to Grace. 'Now you can take your pills if you need them.'

'I can walk a little bit,' Grace protested. 'Dr Grant got me a stick for walking.' She pointed to a crutch leaning against the wall. 'I can still mind Cassie.'

The child was already examining Grace's ornaments and photos. 'Who's this a picture of?'

'Put it down, Cassie. You know better than to touch other people's things.' She turned back to Grace. 'Cassie will be fine with me. I don't have a lot to do and she can sit with me and draw or something. You just sit still and get better. I'll pop back before I go and make sure you're okay.'

Leo had left the work he wanted her to do on the desk.

There was no note to tell her Grace was incapacitated, so she assumed he didn't know.

It would be just like Grace to let everyone think she was fine. She knew the stress they were all under. Alice hoped Leo had managed to leave without Tiffany having a fight with her mother. Right at this minute, Alice believed he was probably the most stressed of them all.

14

Alice got Cassie settled with a pencil, and markers to colour whatever she drew. A stack of white paper should have kept her quiet, but after an hour the little girl was getting bored.

'Can I have a book to look at, please?'

Distracted, Alice looked up from the laptop she had resting on one end of the desk. Cassie had spread her drawings around and Alice only had a small space to work in. Perhaps she could sit the child on the Chesterfield with a book, she thought hopefully, and give herself more room. Choosing a suitable book from the doctor's collection was quite a challenge, but in the end she found a natural history book with pictures of animals.

Cassie took it grudgingly. 'You said there were books with pictures of dragons.'

Alice closed her eyes. She should never have told Cassie about the Jabberwocky poem. 'Those are Dr Grant's books and they're on the top shelves. I can't reach them.'

'There's a ladder. I can see it over there.' Cassie pointed.

'I don't like ladders. I'm afraid I'll fall so I won't go up them, and you're too little to climb a ladder. Leo said Dr Grant will let you look at the dragon book one day, but he's at the hospital now with Tifffany, so for the moment you'll have to look at the animal pictures. Be a good girl and keep quiet for a little while longer, and then I'll see what I can find you for lunch.'

Alice got on with her work as quickly as she could, hoping to finish before lunchtime. Leo had taken some of her suggestions on board and his heroine, Lyra, now spent less time clad from head to toe in leather. Alice had pointed out to Leo that a leather cat suit was not the most sensible clothing for a girl on a tropical island. He now had Lyra wearing a wrestler-back top and tiny shorts. He had gone into quite a lot of detail about the length of the girl's legs, and Alice decided that if the book were ever made into a film it would be a guaranteed blockbuster.

Cassie had settled herself back at the desk and was busy trying to copy animal pictures from the book. Her elephant looked rather like a pig with a long nose, Alice thought, but on the whole she was doing rather well.

'You stay here,' Alice told her, 'and carry on drawing those wonderful animals while I check on Grace. When I come back we'll get something to eat, but it might only be a sandwich.' As she reached the door she looked back at Cassie, but the child was still engrossed in her drawing. 'If you need me I'll be just down the hallway.'

* * *

Leo turned in to the hospital car park with a sigh of relief. Thank goodness the drive was over. Both he and his mother had tried several times to start a conversation with Tiffany, but each time she only managed a grunt in reply.

He knew she wasn't looking forward to the operation, she was scared she might lose the sight in her eye completely, but he also knew that was a very remote possibility. When he tried to tell her so, she had told him sharply to shut up, so he turned on the radio and simply left her to stew in her own misery.

Once he had managed to find a place to park, he helped Tiffany and his mother out of the car and then followed them, carrying Tiffany's bag. He felt like a bellboy, and the private wing did look more like a hotel than a hospital. It was the first time he had seen the place where his father worked, and he was quite impressed.

They were greeted personally by an attractive receptionist and informed that Dr Grant would meet them in Tiffany's room. The hospital might be state-of-the-art technically, but the en-suite room they entered was nothing like any hospital room he had seen before. Soft curtains fluttered in the breeze from the open window and the bed looked large and comfortable. A flat-screen TV hung on the wall, and there were fresh flowers on a small table. Leo realised that any wiring for the obligatory hospital machinery must be hidden behind false wall panels.

His father came into the room dressed in a suit, and Leo was a little disappointed. He had been expecting a white coat, at least. The doctor looked more like a solicitor than a surgeon. Tiffany was booked in for an MRI and when the results came through, a decision would be made. If the retina was intact she would only be in surgery for a short time, but if more work was needed she might be in the operating room for quite a while.

'Why didn't you do the scan last week?' Caroline complained. 'It seems heartless making Tiffany wait around before her surgery.'

'An MRI last week would only have shown her eye at that particular moment in time,' the doctor told his wife. 'Things could very well have changed by today, and I need to know what I'm dealing with right this minute.' He turned to Tiffany. 'Do you want your mother with you while you have your scan?'

Tiffany shook her head automatically, but then she reached out and caught her mother's hand. 'Yes, please. Stay with me, Mom. I need you with me.' She turned to Leo. 'Thanks for driving us here, Leo, but there's no point you staying now. You might as well go back to the house.'

Feeling completely redundant, Leo walked back to the reception area. He left his mobile phone number with the receptionist and asked to be called when Tiffany went into surgery. He did think of hanging around at the hospital, he had been told there was a good cafeteria, but he needed to see Alice.

What he had been dreading had happened. He was missing her.

He climbed into his car and headed back to the house. Perhaps, while he was driving, he might be able to come to some sort of decision.

* * *

Grace was feeling better and had moved from her chair inside the house to one out on the patio. Double petunias dripped in a pale mauve waterfall over the side of a tub, their heady scent filling the air, and a robin was singing happily in a nearby tree.

'I made soup,' Grace told Alice. 'All in a pot. You just have to cut fresh bread.'

'I'll collect Cassie from the library and then we'll come and eat out here with you, if that's okay. I thought you might like the company.'

Grace nodded. 'I like to see the little one.'

Alice was going to heat the soup and

butter the bread before she went back for Cassie, but she didn't like leaving the child on her own for too long, particularly in Dr Grant's library, so she headed straight back up the hall. She was only a few yards from the front door when it opened and Leo appeared.

She looked at him in shocked surprise. 'What are you doing back here? Is something wrong?'

She imagined the worst; quite sure something awful must have happened during Tiffany's operation.

'No, nothing's wrong.' He gave her a rueful grin. 'Tiff kicked me out of the hospital. Her mother is with her and there was nothing for me to do except sit around, so I came back here to see how you were getting on.'

'I'm fine, but did you know Grace has hurt her back?'

'The same old problem?' He sighed when Alice nodded. 'It gets really bad sometimes. I know my father had the best people look at it, but there's nothing much anyone can do. There's an operation she could have, but no guarantee it would work, so she won't have it done. If Grace is out of action, it's a good job you didn't bring Cassie with you.'

'I did bring her. I had to. Lauren had an important client and couldn't look after her. She's drawing pictures in the study.'

Leo frowned. 'You left her alone?'

Now he was criticising the way she looked after her niece. 'Cassie's fine,' Alice said defensively. 'I only popped out to make sure Grace was okay.'

Leo followed Alice into the library and looked around. 'Where is she, then?'

Alice stared at the empty desk. Cassie's drawings were still strewn across the top. 'I've only been gone a few minutes.'

A small sound made them both turn at the same moment. Cassie was at the very top of the rolling ladder, her head nearly touching the high ceiling. She looked guiltily down at Alice and took both hands off the ladder to hold up a book.

'This is the book you told me about, Aunty Alice. The one with the dragon.' Still clutching the book she looked at the floor, a good ten feet below. 'Can you help me down, please?'

'Don't move, Cassie,' Leo said calmly. 'Put the book down and stand still.' He looked at Alice. 'The ladder is supposed to be anchored. If she tries to come down now it could slide away from her. I'm just going to fix the ladder so it can't move,' he called to Cassie, 'and then I'm going to climb up and get you.'

Alice could see it wasn't going to work because Cassie wasn't going to let go of the book. The little girl turned to face Leo, still holding the book with both hands, and for a moment she balanced on the top rung. Then the ladder slid out from under her and she toppled head first towards the floor.

Alice tried to move but her legs

seemed fixed to the floor. Everything happened in slow motion as Cassie fell. The book sailed into the air as the ladder flew along the shelves and banged into the far wall, and then Leo was running forward holding out his arms. Alice watched Cassie slam into him. She was no lightweight and he lost his balance, sitting down hard on the wooden floor, but he still had the little girl cradled in his arms. Alice was about to breathe a sigh of relief when the book Cassie had been holding followed her down, landing with a resounding thump on the top of her head. She stared at Alice for a moment and then her lip started to tremble.

'The book hurt me.'

Leo rocked her in his arms. 'Shush, Cassie. You're fine. I caught you. Just a little bump on the head, that's all.'

Cassie gave him a small, tremulous smile, but when she put a hand to her head and saw a spot of blood she started to cry.

Alice took her niece from Leo,

thanking him with her eyes. What could have been a disaster had been turned in to a minor mishap. If Leo hadn't walked in at the front door at that precise moment, Cassie would have been seriously injured. Alice knew she could never have got to the child in time.

Shaking, she sat on the Chesterfield and hugged Cassie, grateful for the guardian angel that was obviously watching over them. Never again would she leave the little girl alone.

Leo picked himself up from the floor and bent to retrieve the book. It had fallen open, and he smiled when he looked at the page. The Jabberwock stared back at him with eyes of flame.

He showed Cassie the picture. 'I think I just rescued you from the dragon.'

Cassie beamed at him, the pain in her head forgotten. 'That's what a prince is supposed to do.' She looked worried. 'I've put my blood on the book. Will Dr Grant be cross with me?'

'No. He won't be cross. He'll just be glad we outwitted the dragon. Let me look at your head and see if you need a plaster.' He eased Cassie's hair away and found a small puncture wound. 'That's strange. I don't know how the book could make a mark like that.'

'It was one of the dragon's claws,' Cassie said, matter-of-factly. 'I think I do need a plaster.'

'Of course you do,' Leo agreed. 'That's a battle wound.'

A tapping noise made them both turn round. Grace was standing in the doorway, leaning on her crutch. 'What happen?'

Cassie slipped off Alice's lap and ran to Grace. 'I fell off the ladder and got hurt by the dragon. He was trying to kill me and he stuck his claw in my head. The prince saved me, but I need a plaster for my battle wound.'

Grace held out her hand. 'Come. I have a plaster, but I think a brave warrior needs a bandage.' She looked at Alice. 'A plaster will stick to her hair.'

Leo nodded. 'Thank you, Grace. Are you sure you can manage? Don't make your back worse.'

Grace gave him a contemptuous look and hobbled out of the room on her crutch, holding Cassie with her free hand.

'They'll be fine,' he said, sitting on the sofa next to Alice. 'Grace will take good care of her.' He rubbed his chest. 'I think I've got a bruise where Cassie's feet caught me. She was heavier than I thought she was going to be.'

Alice couldn't help smiling. 'It was the speed she was travelling. She hit you like a rocket-driven missile. I'll never forget the look on your face as you sat down on the floor.' She put her hand on his. 'Seriously though, I can never thank you enough. You probably stopped her being seriously hurt.'

'My good deed for the day.' He turned to face her and his eyes held hers. 'I didn't come back here just to see how much work you've got through. I came to tell you I'm not going back to

LA. You're absolutely right, Alice. Tiffany has got to stop leaning on me and learn how to manage on her own. My mother is sitting beside Tiff's bed at the hospital, holding her hand and telling her that she's going to be okay — and that's her job, not mine. That's why I'm not going back to America. I need to be somewhere that Tiff can't simply call me to come over whenever she likes.'

Alice tried to work out what he was telling her. He hadn't decided to stay in England so he could be with her; he was staying in England to get away from Tiffany. It meant the redhead was still calling the shots.

'That's nice,' Alice told him as she got to her feet. 'I don't want to leave Cassie alone with Grace for too long, and I need to get us both something to eat. Have you eaten yet?' She could do the polite and formal thing when she wanted, as well.

She saw him frown. He was probably wondering why she wasn't jumping up and down with delight because he had decided to stay in England.

'I'll come with you. I need to check on Grace as well.'

'Yeah, you do that.' She was feeling really cross with him. If he cared about her at all, he was going to have to tell her. She wasn't in the mind-reading business.

When he reached for her, she moved out of his way. 'Oh, no, you don't. You catch me like that every time. Sometimes kissing isn't enough. I need more than that.'

He raised an eyebrow. 'Are you sure you wouldn't like to rephrase that?'

She felt her face get hot. 'Sarcasm won't work, either.'

'Pity.' He caught her by the shoulders before she could dodge out of his way and turned her to face him. 'What do you want from me, Alice? I can tell you I love you, if that's what you want to hear, but it won't be completely true, because I don't know. I want to be with you every minute of every day, and I want to wake up in the morning with you beside me. I can't go back to America because you won't be with me, and that would be intolerable.'

He slid his hands down her arms and held her wrists. 'Let me ask you a question. Do you love me, Alice?'

She laughed then. 'You've already answered that. I don't know, either.' Pulling her hands free she slid them round his neck and stood on tiptoe to kiss him lightly on the lips. 'But I really want to find out. Come with me to the kitchen and I'll provide you with soup and fresh bread.'

He returned her kiss. 'If that isn't a declaration of love, I don't know what is.'

★   ★   ★

Grace had already set the table in the kitchen and Cassie was sitting on a chair with a large bandage wrapped round her head. 'I'm a warrior,' she said proudly.

As Alice filled her bowl with hot vegetable soup that smelled absolutely wonderful, Leo's phone rang. He pulled it out of his pocket and looked at the screen. 'It's my mother.'

'Well, answer it,' Alice said impatiently.

He held the phone to his ear. 'They've taken Tiff in to surgery. I'd better get back there.'

Grace calmly buttered a slice of warm bread and put it down, melting irresistibly, beside his untouched bowl of soup.

'Eat,' she said. 'A few minutes make no difference.'

'She's right,' put in Alice. And if we're coming with you, Cassie needs to eat as well. So do I, for that matter.'

He sighed. 'I guess you're right.' He picked up his spoon and looked at Alice. 'Are you sure you want to come with me?'

'If we won't get in the way. I'd like Tiffany to know that we care about her.'

Grace hobbled across to top up his

soup bowl and Leo touched her hand.

'I'm not going back to America, Grace. I'm staying in England. I shall live here with my father until I can find a place of my own.'

Grace finished pouring the soup and put the ladle back in the pot. 'You'll stay here? In this house? How long?'

Leo shook his head. 'I don't know. But when I leave, I won't be moving far away. I need to keep an eye on Princess Cassie and make sure she doesn't fall off any more ladders.'

'You have to watch the dragon doesn't get me again.'

'I certainly do. I need to keep your aunty close, as well, to make sure she doesn't disappear down a rabbit hole, like Alice in the book.'

'You stay here because of Alice,' Grace said. A statement, not a question. 'Your mother and the girl, they go back?'

'Tiffany. She does have a name, Grace.' A few days ago he would have been annoyed, but now it amused him.

He got up and put an arm round Grace. 'I'm staying because of you and your cooking. I can't get soup like this in Los Angeles.'

Grace pulled away from him. 'Silly nonsense,' she said, but Alice could see tears in her eyes.

'You take care now,' Leo told her. 'No running around getting dinner. My father is going to keep Tiff overnight at the hospital and my mother will want to stay with her, so you'll only have yourself to worry about.' He picked Cassie up in his arms. 'I'm taking Alice and this little princess to the hospital and then we'll have dinner out somewhere.' He gave Grace a kiss on the cheek. 'I'll be back later — so don't think you've got rid of me.'

Alice persuaded Cassie to remove the bandage before they left. 'If the doctor thinks you're badly wounded, he might want you to stay at the hospital.' She didn't want to frighten the child about going into hospital, but couldn't face the thought of all the explanations she would have to give.

'I don't want your sister to think we're setting up in competition,' she told Leo lightly. 'Cassie can have her bandage back on when she gets home.'

15

Tiffany was lying on the bed when they walked into the room. She waved a limp hand. 'I'm supposed to keep my head still for hours and I'm getting a pain in my neck already,' she said fretfully. 'I'm really hungry, but they won't let me eat anything yet. They gave me something in a syringe to keep my blood-sugar levels up, but it's not the same as a burger and fries.'

'How did it go?' Leo asked his mother.

'As far as I know everything went according to plan, but that's all your father would say. Have a word with him, Leo. He might tell you more than he's told me.'

'He probably doesn't know anything himself. Even if the operation went perfectly, he won't know if Tiff is going to have better sight in that eye for a few weeks yet. He explained all that beforehand, Mother.'

'I know. I'm trying to be positive, but it's really hard. I just want to take Tiffany home.' She gave Alice a weak smile. 'Thank you for coming.'

Cassie had been quiet, but now she was staring at the pink patch over Tiffany's eye with a worried expression. 'Has Dr Grant taken your eye away?'

'Of course not!' Caroline responded in shocked surprise, but Tiffany gave an unexpected snort of laughter.

'If he did, he didn't tell me.' She put a hand to the patch. 'No, it's still there, Cassie. Just covered up until it gets better.'

Leo sat on the side of his sister's bed. 'I'm not coming back home with you, Tiff. Mother will look after you, she's been wanting to do that for years, and once you have your sight back you'll be busy modelling again. I'll have to come back in a couple of weeks to collect all my stuff, but then I'm going to stay over here and find somewhere to live. I think we always have a connection to the place where we were born.' He held up his hand, alarmed, as Tiffany stirred on her pillows. 'Don't try and sit up. You'll undo all the work you've just had done.'

Tiffany didn't get a chance to answer, as Caroline was already on her feet. 'Don't do this now, Leo! Your sister has been through enough. Don't you think you owe her a little of your time? She's relying on you.'

'I know,' he said quietly. He took Tiffany's hand. 'You've grown into a beautiful woman, Tiff, and you're quite capable of looking after yourself. You have to keep on top of your diabetes, but thousands of people live with it every day of their lives and don't allow it to spoil anything. That part is up to you.'

Tiffany slid her unaffected eye sideways and smiled at Alice. 'He's staying because of you, isn't he? Take care of him. He's the only brother I've got.'

Cassie climbed up on the bed and lay down beside Tiffany. 'Don't worry, I'll look after him for you,' she said confidently, patting her hand.

'I hope you're not upsetting my patient,' Dr Grant said from the doorway. 'I've organised some food for you, Tiffany, and you can start moving around a bit. Just don't do anything suddenly.'

He held out his hand to Cassie. 'Down you come, little one — only one patient is allowed in a bed in my hospital.'

Cassie climbed down reluctantly. 'If Tiffany had a black patch she'd look like a pirate.'

Leo picked the little girl up and sat her on his hip. 'I think we'd better go and let you have your lunch, Tiff.' He turned to his father. 'Are you keeping her in overnight?'

The doctor nodded. 'Yes. Just to be on the safe side. She can go home tomorrow morning, after I've checked her over.'

'I'm staying tonight,' Caroline said. 'Peter has organised a bed for me here.'

★ ★ ★

Cassie sat on her booster seat in the back of Leo's car on the ride home, playing her new computer game. Alice sent up a silent thanks for technology. She wanted to talk to Leo.

'Are you sure this is what you want, Leo? Tiffany thinks you're staying in England because of me and I don't want that sort of responsibility. If you regret it, you'll blame me.'

'If I regret it after a few months I'll go back to LA. I make my own decisions, Alice. At the moment I want to be here with you, and I want Tiff and my mother to learn how to get along.'

He took his eyes off the road for a second to look at her.

'A mother and daughter should get along, shouldn't they?'

Alice sighed. 'Thousands don't, but yes, they should, and maybe with no big

309

brother to rely on, Tiffany may find that she needs her mother.'

'That's exactly what I thought.' He raised his eyes to look in the rear-view mirror. 'I was going to treat you both to dinner, but Cassie appears to have gone to sleep.'

Alice turned round. It always amazed her how children could drift off to sleep perched on a booster seat. 'Come in and have something to eat with me and Lauren. She'll have cooked, anyway, and you told Grace not to get anything ready for you.'

Lauren greeted them and Leo carried a sleepy Cassie into the house. Joe, sitting on the sofa, obligingly made room for her.

'I fell off the ladder,' Cassie told him. 'Then the dragon put his claw in me and made my head bleed.' She gave her mother a big smile. 'But the prince saved me.'

Alice sighed. 'See? This is why I made Cassie take her bandage off.'

'She had a bandage on?' Lauren said

worriedly. 'Exactly how bad was this dragon wound?'

'It was very serious,' Leo said with a wink at Lauren. 'After all, it was made by a dragon. I think Cassie needs her bandage back on now.'

Alice handed Leo the bandage and followed Lauren into the kitchen, shutting the door behind them. 'It was only a tiny scratch, Lauren, but it was my fault and I'm really sorry. Grace hurt her back so I had to keep Cassie with me. I left her alone in the library for just a moment and she climbed up a ladder and fell off. Leo caught her, but she landed with both feet on his chest, so I think he came off worst.'

Lauren gave Alice a hug. 'Oh, you poor thing. I would have cancelled if I'd known Grace was ill. Cassie can be a nightmare sometimes. She's old enough to know how to behave herself.'

'She was just behaving like a child. It wasn't her fault. Usually she's as good as gold.' Alice looked at the saucepan Lauren was stirring. 'Bolognaise? Will there be enough for Leo?'

'Of course there will. I asked Joe to stay, so I made heaps, and I have garlic bread and a salad to go with the pasta.'

Alice glanced at the closed door. 'Leo's going to stay in England, Lauren.' She wriggled out of her sister's enthusiastic hug as the door opened and Joe stuck his head in.

'Shall we set the table while you two are nattering?'

'We, as in who?'

'Me and Leo. He's just told me he's staying here in England, so he's got to learn the rules. If the women cook dinner, the men have to set the table and load the dishwasher.' He grinned at them both. 'And vice versa, of course.'

Lauren handed him forks. 'Your turn to cook next time, then.'

'I was just saying to Leo we ought to try that new restaurant down . . . ' He ducked as Lauren threw a spoon at him. 'Or we could team up and do our best to rustle up a halfway decent meal for you both.'

'Actually, the restaurant idea sounds good,' Alice joked.

The meal was fun. Cassie went to bed, and they sat talking until Leo said he had better get home and check on Grace.

'Why don't you come round in the morning and say hello to Tiffany?' he asked Alice. 'She'll still have to wear her patch, but she should be feeling better and we'll know how soon she can fly back home.'

Once the men had gone, Lauren wanted to know everything. Why Leo had decided to stay, how Tiffany was getting on, and exactly what Cassie had been up to. Alice pleaded tiredness, but wasn't allowed to go to bed until Lauren was fully satisfied.

'How about you?' Alice asked her. 'How did your day go?'

'I don't suppose you want to know about my client, do you? Although she has told me I will definitely get all six bridesmaids to beautify when she gets married.'

Lauren twisted her hands together in her lap. 'I sort of let slip that I might quite like another baby and Joe said that I'd better make it soon or I'd be too old. Tact isn't in his vocabulary.'

'And?' Alice asked impatiently.

'Well . . . he asked me to marry him, so I suppose that means we're sort of unofficially engaged.' Lauren smiled uncertainly.

'We're doing a lot of hugging today,' Alice said, when she eventually let her sister go. 'The men couldn't drink tonight because they were both driving, but there's nothing to stop us.'

They finished half a bottle of Chardonnay between them, and Alice slept soundly until her alarm went off. She made sure that Lauren could manage Cassie on her own, and then drove round to the doctor's house. She had been hoping she would get there before Tiffany and her mother arrived, so she could have some time alone with Leo, but the doctor's car was already parked in the driveway.

Leo greeted her with a smile and a kiss. 'The one I couldn't give you last night because your sister was watching,' he said. 'Tiffany is feeling great. There should be no problem with the eye. She can get checked over when she gets home and my father thinks the other eye only needs laser treatment. She's going home with my mother the day after tomorrow.'

'How about you?' Alice asked. 'You said you need to go back to pick up your things.'

He put his arm round her shoulders, stopping her from going any further into the house. 'We've had a talk this morning, before you arrived, and we've come up with a plan. I'm not going back with my mother and Tiffany. I'm going to leave it a couple of weeks and then fly out to arrange for any important stuff to be shipped back here.' He took a breath and reached for her hands. 'I want you to come with me, Alice. You'll still be on vacation from school and I thought we might take Cassie as well. I want to show her Disneyland.'

Alice felt her heart skip a beat. 'Lauren won't want to miss Cassie's first trip to Disneyland. Could she come as well? I'm sure she can cancel any appointments she has for a few days.'

Leo lifted Alice off her feet. 'And Joe! Let's take him too.'

Alice slid out of his arms, feeling her excitement ebb as reality kicked in. She was getting carried away.

'It would be wonderful, Leo — but we can't afford a trip like that. The boiler still has to be fixed.'

'Do this for me, Alice. I'm happy to pay for you all, and I want to see Cassie's face when she meets the real Sleeping Beauty and Prince Charming. Don't take that away from me.'

She knew he could afford it. That wasn't the problem. She just needed a good reason to say yes.

'Lauren and Joe got engaged last night,' she said casually. 'She might just agree to come with us if you tell her it's an engagement present. And I think I deserve a bonus for all the work I've done for you — so you can pay for my flight out of that.'

He beamed in satisfaction. 'Agreed. But I need a kiss to seal the deal.' As she moved towards him, he murmured thoughtfully, 'Joe's a clever guy and getting engaged is a pretty cool idea. I'll have to think about that one.'

Alice smiled and slid her arms round his neck. 'How about we leave the thinking for later? One important thing at a time . . . '

THE END

We do hope that you have enjoyed reading this large print book.

Did you know that all of our titles are available for purchase?

We publish a wide range of high quality large print books including:
Romances, Mysteries, Classics General Fiction Non Fiction and Westerns

Special interest titles available in large print are:
The Little Oxford Dictionary Music Book, Song Book Hymn Book, Service Book

Also available from us courtesy of Oxford University Press:
Young Readers' Dictionary (large print edition) Young Readers' Thesaurus (large print edition)

For further information or a free brochure, please contact us at:
**Ulverscroft Large Print Books Ltd., The Green, Bradgate Road, Anstey, Leicester, LE7 7FU, England.
Tel:** (00 44) **0116 236 4325
Fax:** (00 44) **0116 234 0205**

AS TIME GOES BY

Gillian Villiers

When Lally caretakes her grand-mother's croft in the wildest part of Scotland, she fully expects that she'll return soon, to a high-powered job in Edinburgh. Her scatterbrained sister Bel has other plans though, and Lally quickly finds the people and the place seeping into her soul. Or is it just one person, in the shape of new neighbour Iain? Torn between two worlds, Lally's decision will not only impact on herself, but also on everyone else around her.

A CERTAIN SMILE

Beth James

Freya has been made redundant and her high-flying boyfriend, Jay, is pressurising her to join him in London. But this would mean her leaving the place her heart lies — her home in the New Forest. And there are so many things to consider: her friends, her small cottage and her adorable, little dog Henri . . . and there's a certain dog walker with good legs and a friendly smile. Freya knows that she'd miss saying 'good morning' to him too.

CORY'S GIRLS

Teresa Ashby

Mark Jacobs returns to his home town to settle old scores, but learns that his ex-wife died two years before. Emma, his daughter from that marriage, and with whom he'd lost contact, is settled and happy with Cory Elliot, her stepfather, and her two half-sisters. But Mark wants her back, and when Cory has to go abroad on business, he leaves the girls with Katrina, who has to fight to keep the family together for Cory — the man she loves.

WHERE LOVE BELONGS

Chrissie Loveday

Lizzie Vale, Nellie Cobridge's youngest sibling, has to make a decision. What will she do with her life? Journalism excites her, but in 1938 it's not easy for a woman to get a job in this field, however bright and lively she is. Determined to succeed, she tries various schemes and tackles everything with enthusiasm. Fortunately, she has the support of a loving family when things go wrong. She meets Charlie and her future seems set. Or is it?